QUEEN PALM

SAM MOSSLER

First edition

ISBN-13: 978-1-956672-97-8 (Paperback edition)

ISBN-13: 978-1-956672-96-1 (Ebook edition)

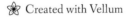 Created with Vellum

STORIES TAKE FLIGHT AT IBIS BOOKS

STORIES FOR READERS, RESOURCES FOR WRITERS

The IBIS is sacred to Thoth, the Egyptian god of learning, inventor of writing, and scribe to the gods.

They are gregarious birds that live, travel, and breed in flocks.

And they are legendary for their courage.

Visit ibis-books.com to purchase more stories and learn how to publish your own!

Build yourself a rocket ship to Mars.
Travel round the world in flying cars.
Try your best to not go starting wars
and keep evolving, please.

Get some eggs and flour and bake a cake.
Figure out that life is give and take.
Just don't throw your garbage in the lake
and keep evolving, please.

It isn't always clear
What we're doing here,
That's the bummer of free will.
But you can be sure
If your heart is pure
Of life's joy you'll have your fill.

Travel round the world and study rocks.
Make your living selling bonds and stocks.
But never stuff your life-force in a box
and keep evolving, please.

Keep evolving, please.

SAM MOSSLER

CONTENTS

FOREWORD

Sam Mossler wore a fedora, jacket, and tie to his first day of 6th Grade at Booker Middle School in Sarasota, Florida. It was 1986. He carried a briefcase stuffed with papers, pens, sketches he was writing, faces he was drawing, and the script to *Little Shop of Horrors*. He'd very recently turned 11 and he was already a fully formed person—the first I ever met who was my age or younger.

I was 13 and it was my first day of 8th grade. I was wearing an Izod polo, grey corduroy shorts, athletic socks, and some generic tennis shoes. I don't think they had Velcro on them. It wasn't technically a uniform, but everybody was wearing it.

Booker Middle's school day ended at 2:45. Sam took the High School bus home at 3:30. My mother taught math at Booker High School. So Sam and I and five or six other students were held in Study Hall from 2:45 to 3:30 every day. Mr. Frank was more than happy to let us huddle up with our friends and talk quietly.

We fell in together. Sam immediately invited me to create with him. He invited everyone to create with him. For 45 minutes every day after school, we worked through *Little Shop* and *Saturday Night Live*, Louis Prima, Tom Lehrer, and Mel Brooks. I was in Ms. Ferguson's drama class, and it was great, and Sam already knew everything about theatre somehow. We wrote sketches, songs, and short stories. We talked about the art we loved, the art we were making, the art we wanted to make. Study Hall may have been the best class I took in 8th Grade. It was the most formative.

Sam was funny without being mean.

He was confident without being arrogant.

He was kind without being soft.

He was wise without being pedantic.

He leaned in to listen to everybody.

And he tells a really good story.

Josh Ford
October 22, 2021

—————

When Sam wrote, he didn't only write words. He created worlds. Places of wonder and whimsy. Anecdotal and absurd. Poignant and passionate. And his worlds weren't merely written down, but they transgressed into the reality he inhabited. Sam was one of the most welcoming humans I ever met. And he shared all the things he loved.

If it wasn't for Sam, I would never have been introduced to incalculable elements that formed my foundation as an artist and a person. Theatre, literature, cinema, how to construct the perfect dirty limerick... and so on. His taste in music alone; eclectic beyond reckoning. If not for Sam, I would have absolutely no concept of the brilliance of so many musicians. He made the most amazing mixtapes. Yes, the cassette kind. As technology advanced, they became mix-CDs. A yearly tradition was the much anticipated *Fourth of July Mix*, celebrating that current number of years of Independence. It without fail included The Police's *Roxanne* (a drinking song of much renown in our friend circles).

We wrote together. A lot. And though our literary voices were by no means exactly the same (his grasp on vocabulary and use of pulchritudinous words far exceeded mine), we had a certain melodic style. Sam and I knew the tune and harmonized together beautifully. We would sit in smoky dive bars and write "Bar Napkin Beat Poetry." There was a writing form that we aptly called "Pass the Pad," where one of us would begin writing something on a yellow line-ruled pad (a must-have creative tool), be it a scene, short story, or existential musing. Then we would pass the pads between ourselves, sometimes when still halfway through a thought, leaving the other to pick up where it was left off.

I believe we all in some way yearn for a partner in crime. That someone who *gets* you. Accepts you. Follies, foibles, and all. What one might call, for lack of a better word, a soulmate. People can search their entire lives for that someone that they can connect with, complain to, confide in, and essentially complete you. I was extremely fortunate. I found that person when I was 9 years old.

I will close with some words I found in one of Sam's (copious) journals. I'm sure for him it was just "filler." A quick thought that creeped out of his head and onto the paper. And as I write this, I can hear his voice saying: "Really, Rat? That's what you're going to use?" But I think it shows that Sam's brilliance is eternal. So it goes.

Adam Ratner
October 22, 2021

"Time has very little to do with wisdom. Wisdom has very little to do with beauty. Time eats beauty. Wisdom eats time. Wisdom, however indirectly, eats beauty. So if you want to maintain your beauty try not thinking so much."

Sam Mossler

July 5, 2010

PREFACE

Greetings, Reader. My name is Jason Cannon. I am not the author, but it falls to me to write this preface because the last several months I've had the wonderful pleasure of splashing around inside the mind of Sam Mossler, who was unfairly taken from this world almost exactly a year ago. It is one of the honors of my life that his family and partner gave me their blessing to finish and publish his debut novel.

Queen Palm the novel started out as *The Solfeggio Project* the screenplay. A couple of months into lockdown, call it the summer of 2020, a few friends and associates started a weekly Saturday online writing club. We read each other's stuff, gave each other feedback and encouragement, and came to rely on each other's imaginations and creativity as an escape from the craziness of the world. You could think of us as modern-day Inklings, only our pub was a Zoom room. And from that writing club of yore, we pulled our name, the Rabbit Room, which is the room inside The Eagle and Child public house where JRR Tolkien, CS Lewis, and their gang would meet. And drink, dammit.

We shared poetry, short stories, comedic essays, sketches, plays. After years of talking about it but never doing it, I finally assayed a novel, and it is no exaggeration to say my debut thriller, *Ghost Light*, would not exist without the assistance and guidance of Sam and the Rabbit Room. He and they were the most generous and insightful of cheerleaders.

Sam was about 80% of the way through adapting his screenplay into this novel when he simply didn't wake up one morning in late 2020.

I finished my book, published it, and dedicated it to Sam. Discovered how much I love writing and publishing. Got the OK from Sam's nearest and dearest to take a crack at finishing his book. Realized the best way to do so would be to form a publishing company. Thus did Ibis Books come to be. Ibis Books, in a very real way, is an ongoing testament to the singular, wacky, wonderful mind of Sam Mossler.

I had all of Sam's chapters from his time sharing in the Rabbit Room. His partner Nicole did the heart-rending work of digging through his yellow legal pad notes and computer files and sent me his most up-to-date musings on the story. His brother Mickey sent me the full original screenplay, which provided the final keys to the narrator, climax, and denouement. I started by pulling plot points and dialogue directly from the screenplay. I went back to Chapter One and stepped through, scrubbing continuity and applying notes Sam had inserted throughout his various manuscripts. At all times I tried to work from primary source material, and made edits or additions only when it seemed necessary for flow or clarity, and even then only when I felt confident I had discerned Sam's intent and trajectory. I tried to think of my role less as ghostwriter or even editor and more as sculptor, carefully chipping and brushing away to *discover* Sam's book rather than invent it.

That being said, any mistakes in here are totally on me.

So that's how *Queen Palm* came together. But I'd be remiss if I didn't share a bit more about Sam himself.

First, he made a killer Old Fashioned. I know this first hand.

Second, he was my partner in crime when it came to the Florida Studio Theatre School. I oversee the classes and instructors, and I leaned heavily on Sam as a playwriting teacher.

Third and most special, he and I were theatrical muses for each other. I got to direct Sam four times, starting with *How to Use a Knife* in 2018. Then *Other People's Money*, *The Nether*, and finally *Kunstler*.

During *How to Use a Knife*, Sam and I figured each other out. Learned we could both bring our strongest ideas to rehearsal and smash them together and trust each other implicitly. His character, Chef George, was often referred to as "Jefe" by other characters in the play. And thus did Sam call me "Jefe" ever after.

Sam was such a gentle and laid-back soul, grounded and calm. Yet Chef George was a volcano with a seething, rotten, desperate core. And when Sam accessed those deepest truths within himself, he was transcendent on stage.

No more so than in *Kunstler*. It was obvious Sam was great for it when he auditioned. It was also obvious he was, oh, thirty years too young for the role! Not even an hour after his callback —and Sam knew he had nailed it—I got an email from him. He had sent me his headshot, photoshopped with gray hair and gray eyebrows and wrinkles. He wrote simply, "Just in case."

I wish all of you reading right now could have seen *Kunstler* because Sam was, again, transcendent. The play is mostly a direct-address monologue, pages and pages of politics and stories and history. Rehearsal was a special time, because so often it was just him and me, slogging up this mountain of text.

He'd finish a scene, after we had pushed past what we *thought* he could do to what we *discovered* he could do, and he'd sit, his armpits swampy and his brow dripping, and he'd look at me, and crack his iconic chuckling smile, the one where his eyes crinkled. He was wrung out, but he was exactly where he wanted to be.

Kunstler closed the day before Florida Studio Theatre had to shut down operations due to the pandemic. Sam's performance was the last to grace our stages, until we were able to reopen over a year later. A few weeks after closing, he and I were talking on Zoom. And I swear to you this is the absolute truth. Sam said to me, "Jefe, this run of roles I've had at FST the last couple years... It's been unbelievable. And *Kunstler*, I'm so grateful I got to do that, and to finish the run. It was like summiting Everest. I don't think anything could ever top it. Honestly, if I never get to act again... I'm happy."

This is how I remember Sam. The last scene of *Kunstler*, the activist lawyer speaks to us from beyond the grave, telling us that *no no no you still don't understand*. And after Sam booms out that line, he strides onto the stage, hits his mark in a spotlight, smiles, and opens his arms so incredibly wide. To hug the young lawyer character across from him, to hug all of us in the audience, to hug the world.

It is infuriating, and unfair, and makes no sense, but the transcendent Sam Mossler never got to act again.

But I am comforted by that image. Sam is in the spotlight. And he is smiling, with crinkled eyes. And his arms are open wide.

And he is happy.

I hope to all things holy that wherever my friend is, he is pleased with *Queen Palm*.

1

THE PONTUS SUPREME B-15

The offshore rig, named Pontus Supreme B-15, emitted significantly less noise at night, but in no way did this suggest that the crew found much time to sleep. If you were to hover over the Gulf at around midnight on any given night, you would hear the din of late-night carousing from as far as a half-mile away from the rig.

On this particular night, you would first hear, whether you liked it or not, Blues Traveler. And as you glided closer you would hear occasional whoops and whelps and curses and laughter. And if you floated down the galley and into the interior of the rig's living quarters, 'neath the strident harmonica and boisterous cheers you would hear the recurring sound of a ping pong ball being hit across a table.

Come along, now. There's no danger. At least not to you.

Inside the Pontus Supreme B-15, its employee pool—welders, mechanics, engineers, drillers, roustabouts, rig operators, and roughnecks—were putting their deep-earth plunders behind them with a late-night buffet and table tennis tournament. Those who hadn't lost interest in (or had money riding on) the outcome of the game watched the little white orb bouncing back and forth while their baked ziti digested.

Suddenly a single thud shook the room. All the noises stopped except for the clatter of the abruptly abandoned ping pong ball traversing the floor. In short order, all of the lights got very bright and each of the denizens of that insidious floating city became sensually attuned to the pungent, chemical fumes in their mouths, noses, and eyes. A few of the more prescient operators immediately jetted. The majority just stood there, gasping and coughing. Then the walls began to shake. En masse the crew crammed itself through the narrow doors into the cramped hall and up the stifling stairs.

Amid this frantic exodus, the gas—which had cleverly escaped from the mud treatment modules—migrated to the HVAC inlets, found blessed ignition at the hands of an 11Kv switchboard, and turned from not-so-noble gas into mighty, malevolent hellfire with one of the most impressive explosions that e'er invention played on.

The men and women who'd escaped to the deck now sloshed around the muddy surface desperately attempting to locate their designated lifeboats. Their only light source: a roaring pillar of flame towering over the entire rig. Their clumsy escapes were further hampered when the reserves of diesel and helicopter fuel joined the blazing pageant, rending asunder all who remained.

For its glorious grand finale, the gas found a most fertile source of ignition in the emergency generator. The ensuing fulmination rendered the whole shebang—the entire six-hundred-million-dollar platform—non-existent. Save for the dainty parachutes of flame that fluttered down toward the sea, there was no indication that there had ever been a Pontus Supreme B-15.

2

THE DEBATE

A few hours before the Pontus Supreme B-15 ceased to be, a dated civic auditorium at a carefully selected public university was all abuzz with preparations for the first televised debate between one of the major party's nominees, such as they were, for Governor of the great state of Florida.

Each candidate, with one exception, was grappling with enormous personal issues. Issues that had nothing to do with their candidacies, per se. Issues that could befall a person in any walk of life, but just so happened to befall this collection of candidates standing behind a semi-circle of podiums on a meticulously arranged stage in front of a thoroughly vetted and curated crowd.

The most apparent personal issue was, of course, the only one that had been made public. This was the revelation that Lindsey Swallerman, Congresswoman from District 3, had a daughter employed by an S&M dungeon in New Orleans. Naturally, this seamy discovery had great political consequence, especially since Swallerman's so-north-it's-south Panhandle constituency leaned hard starboard on social, cultural, and familial issues. Her soaring political career that until yesterday had seemed destined for numerous future nominations was coming in for a bumpy landing indeed.

All that aside, Congresswoman Swallerman truly was enduring profound shock, as by all reports her daughter had been studying theology and athletics at Tulane but upon further investigation had been discovered to be making a decent living in the kink industry. And every proverb, moral lesson, etiquette enforcement, gentle nudge, in fact every loving act of parenting undertaken over the span of eighteen years had been undone in a matter of months and cast aside like a sweaty vinyl bustier.

Lindsey Swallerman was broken. Yet an effete young man, most likely with problems of his own, dutifully powdered the Congresswoman's nose while she stared directly over her podium into the blinding glare of destiny's taillights.

To her left was the tub of sweat whom Jacksonville called "Mayor." Wesley Schla was not the smartest candidate, nor the most charismatic, nor the most politically savvy, nor the most rational, nor the most likely to help a friend move into a new apartment. Nor would he likely be able to name the delineation of powers and responsibilities implicit in the executive, legislative, and judicial branches. Nor could he refrain from biting his fingernails or making fool's bets or behaving abominably on airplanes.

What Mayor Schla was very good at was going to extraordinarily great lengths, often winding and arbitrary, in order to make a point or appear correct. And the fact was that his entire candidacy was a premeditated attempt to prove his father wrong. About everything.

But the polls were dismal. So much so that when another candidate made an early departure from the race, the media delighted in pointing out that his numbers were still better than Schla's.

They also made fun of his name. *Schlaaaa*. One flippant member of the press had posited that "a distant ancestor must have abruptly dropped dead in the middle of a census interview." They were having a field day with Schla, alright.

All the tension about his unsatisfying public persona and his smug father and his lack of credentials and his stupid name had conspired to form a karmic tumor that manifested in the form of a very noticeable stammer. It had begun three weeks ago, shortly after lunch, during an interview with a high school newspaper in West Palm Beach. Schla was discussing his favorite hobby, fly fishing, and he suddenly found he couldn't say "lure." He tried twice and nothing came out. But he refused to give up and emitted a train of strident "L-L-L-L-L-L-L-L's." This went on for literally three minutes and the student editor went from uncomfortable to miserable as Schla implored her patience by saying "P-P-p-p-P-p-P-P-P!" His aide ushered the young journalist out of the room and gave her a tote bag.

In the passing days, Schla had been unable to muster a single consistently coherent word except for "FUCK!"

And now the moderator was greeting the audience of millions and nobody knew who would be called on first. Mayor Schla whimpered. Audibly.

This caught the attention of the old silverback, Pat Lueke, arranging his notes with typical corner-crinkling force. He spoke with patronizing mock concern, as if he'd never seen a statesman in the middle of a meltdown.

"Everything okay, Wes?"

Schla looked at him like he had just wet his pants. Hell, maybe he had.

"Pull it together, boy."

Schla shuddered. The motion sent pellets of perspiration every which way.

The moderator ran down the rules of the debate. As futile as such rules ultimately were on a stage full of megalomaniacs, narcissists, and sociopaths, the network insisted. They felt it gave the symposium at least the appearance of credibility.

As he listened to the rules being read, Pat Lueke licked his lips in anticipation. He was gonna break every last goddamn one of 'em. After all, if anyone had the right to do so, by virtue of their sheer, demented pomposity, it was Lueke. What everyone present knew, except Lueke himself, was that his campaign was merely symbolic. What everyone didn't know— what only Lueke and his cardiologist knew—was that his heart, pummeled with hard living and wanton gorging, could go kaput at any second. He was an ambulatory dead man. But he was going out with six-shooters a-blazin', yee-hawin' with more verbosity and vitriol than he'd shown since the famous 1992 go-around.

Meantime, Arnie Dunne was paying hush money to former lovers, Lenore Pringle was pouring all her resources into keeping her insider-trading charges from the tabloids, Chris Norwood was seriously contemplating going back to school to study modern dance, and Ryan Cannadee had completely run out of funds and would be dropping out of the race the following morning.

Everyone had their emotional plate full.

Except for Congressman Vern Bushnell of the 13th District. Vern Bushnell, mid-50s, not *un*handsome, hair perfectly graying around the edges and resisting time's thinning, still just fit enough that he could button his suit jacket without a struggle, stood relaxed and calm, grounded like a yogi, with the vaguest Mona Lisa smile lifting his lips. On his spray-tanned forehead dwelt nary a bead of sweat. After all,

Vern's candidacy was the surest thing going, the whispered pick in all the sausage-making rooms. The Swallerman girl had simply sealed the deal.

Vern looked out into the buzzing crowd and gave the slightest inclination of his head to his benefactors, the Sneed Brothers, paper and petroleum empire overlords, who owned this night just as much as he did. Their generosity and patriotism had propelled him from shiftless spit-shiner to City Councilman to the State House to Congressional Representative to Gubernatorial Contender in a mere twenty-five years. Not to say Bushnell's easy charm and political acumen didn't play a part. Of course they did.

But it always takes two to tango.

3

VERN BUSHNELL'S HOME DISTRICT

Queen Palm, Florida, spread gradually—like red tide or like compound interest, depending on your point of view—from a single small cottage on an inlet of the Gulf of Mexico in the late 1800's to a sizable city, replete with a Whole Foods and a Sur la Table, in the present.

It hadn't always been called Queen Palm. For the longest time, it was known as Sawnichikee, a sleepy little beach town with a hybrid sensibility. Rednecks happily bred with hippies, former circus performers with drunken Lithuanian abstract expressionists, and mystery novelists with the spring-training roster of the Chicago White Sox.

Vern Bushnell's parents moved to Sawnichikee, as it was still called in 1973, from Dearborn Heights, Michigan. They'd vacationed in Sawnichikee the previous summer, baby Vern in tow, and were enchanted, as most people were. Mary Ann, the soft-spoken mater, hadn't felt so well since she was a teenager. The color came back to her face. Her old sense of humor returned. (She'd always been a witty gal before she started having children.) Artie, the withering pater, almost shuddered when Mary Ann reached across and tousled his hair at the beach one day. She touched him so infrequently back in Michigan. Hardly at all. But in Sawnichikee she was all hands. So affectionate.

A few days before they had to get back in the Country Squire and drive back north, Artie said, "You look good, Mary Ann. You really do."

Mary Ann said, "You don't look so bad, yourself."

And from that moment Artie knew that Sawnichikee would be their home, the Lions and Tigers and Pistons be damned. Less than half a year later an army buddy of Artie's made a few phone calls on Artie's behalf and got him a job at Ed Roast's Ford Dealership in Sawnichikee. "Roast's the Most! On Highway 41!"

Then, right around the time disco was being choked to death by soft rock, the Sneeds showed up. A completely random vacation stop-over abruptly transformed into a scoping-out mission, for the Sneeds, like the locals (which now included the Bushnells), saw the beauty and sincerely got off on the haunted vibe and the lazy afternoons. But whereas the average Sawnichikeeite saw that beauty and thought "this should never end," the Sneeds saw in its purity a profoundly pliable market. They sensed, in its lamentable lack of order, exceptional opportunity to concentrate their wealth and use this quaint wilderness as a laboratory, a testing ground for their global ambitions.

So they set about marketing it.

It took a few years, and more than a few backroom deals sealed with clinking tumblers of the local coconut rum, but they manipulated the city council into agreeing, for the sake of its vital tourism industry, that the city's name be changed from Sawnichikee to something the vacationers would feel comfortable pronouncing at a gas station. And so Sawnichikee became Queen Palm in 1985. A couple of schools, one hardware store, the strip mall closest to the original inlet, and a long-running community theatre held out, retaining "Sawnichikee" in their monikers, but otherwise, there was hardly any sign that it had ever been called anything but Queen Palm. And, if you didn't live there before 1985, it didn't much matter that history meant nothing.

4

VERN MEETS THE SNEEDS

In the early part of a summer in the early 1980s, Vern's father dropped his son into Fortuna's lap. He did so without any awareness of the grave consequences of his actions. In his view, he was simply introducing his son to the notion of an honest living, as would any father worth his neck-tie. He pulled his fresh-from-the-lot Taurus into Johnny's Car Wash, shooed Vern out the door, and drove up 41 to Roast's to punch the clock, leaving his son behind for his first day as a meaningful member of the job force.

Many great things would come from this nascent association. Vern would develop a modicum of competence and a sense of personal responsibility. Vern would lose fifteen pounds. Vern would be able to save up enough money to buy a fixer-upper Z-28.

And Vern would meet the brothers Sneed.

It was mid-August when the Bentley rolled into Johnny's lot and pulled up directly next to the Oldsmobile that Vern was polishing. Vern's jaw and polishing rag dropped simultaneously. Sandy Sneed, perpetual octogenarian and reptilian overlord, stepped out of the car and approached Vern with an otherworldly sense of purpose.

Vern spluttered, "Holy smokes! Is that a Bentley?"

"That it is, young man. Take it in."

"Hot holy Christ..."

Sandy never tired of watching plebeian reactions to gleaming luxuries.

"It has every modern convenience imaginable except, regrettably, the ability to deflect seagull droppings."

Vern saw the crusted heap of white and green dung on the Bentley's hood.

"Oh, man. They got you good, didn't they?" Vern ascertained the bird shit's texture by poking at it with his bare index finger. "How long has it been on there?"

"Possibly as many as three days. My brother and I were away at Hilton Head when it happened."

"Mmmmm. The thing about seagull shit is that it's got all kinds of acid in it. The longer it sits the more damage. What I would do is polish down the paint around it and—"

"How long will that take?"

"Well, sir, I have three cars ahead of you but—"

And then Sandy Sneed blithely passed Vern a one-hundred-dollar bill.

"Half an hour, shall we say?"

Vern didn't splutter. His instincts kicked in and he hopped to. "Yes, SIR!"

Sandy Sneed knocked on the tinted window and his brother Malcolm, lither and somehow leatherier, emerged from the car and opened an umbrella to protect himself from the glare. Vern put the bill in his pocket as he watched the two brothers slither to the shade of Johnny's awning and settle on a bench. Then he abandoned the Oldsmobile and got to work on the Sneeds' Bentley.

Now, the seamless removal of crusty avian excreta from the hood of a luxury automobile may seem like a small accomplishment in the grand scheme of things. But in this case, Vern's mundane acumen was countervailing. Sandy Sneed, notorious for his withering stoicism, was so uncharacteristically moved at the sight of his restored Bentley that he took Vern's hand in both of his, squeezed tightly, and said, "You've done us a great service, son. We will not forget this."

Then he sniffed at his brother and got into the back seat. Taking his elder brother's prompting, Malcolm produced an embossed business card from his breast pocket and handed it to Vern.

"How much do we owe you?" Malcolm asked.

"Well, he already—"

Malcolm slipped Vern another hundred-dollar bill. Vern gaped. Malcolm grinned.

"What's your name, young man?"

"Vern. Vern Bushnell."

"We'll be seeing you around, Vern Bushnell."

Vern stood gobsmacked as he watched the Bentley purr out of the parking lot.

5

THE OLD HEIDELBERG CASTLE, 1984

Vern's Z-28 had sport suspension, dual exhausts, 15x7 wheels, Positraction, a black finish grille, sport mirrors on both sides, front and rear spoilers, and a 350 cubic inch, 245 horsepower V8 engine. He called her "Tina." His favorite pastime was driving shirtless down Tamiami Trail at high speeds with a tallboy of Miller Lite secured between his thighs.

The evening after his initial meeting with the Sneeds, he drove even faster than usual. He played his music even louder than usual. He didn't bother with a tallboy because tonight he was going to drink beer from a goddamn *glass*. He had two hundred-dollar bills in his pocket and he was out for the most raucous divertissement that Sawnichikee had to offer.

Sawnichikee possessed a unique natural resource, owing to its distinctive climate. It was a place where ancient show folk went to die. The folks who got too old to spend another season with the circus stayed behind when the winter ended. And all the session musicians who saved up enough bread to spend their golden years in paradise, but didn't have quite enough for Ft. Myers, invariably ended their migration in Sawnichikee.

This was to the great advantage of a good many local nightspots that offered live entertainment.

The Old Heidelberg Castle featured aged trapeze artists wearing lederhosen hurling through the air while ancient musicians, also lederhosened, played "The Too Fat Polka." The ambiance was heightened by the fact that there weren't a lot of health code considerations back then so the menu featured huge wooden trays of greasy sausages— bratwurst, knockwurst, bockwurst, any wurst you wanted—all washed down with massive steins of Old Style filled from plastic pitchers as indiscriminately as if it were iced tea. Every patron left exhilarated and polluted. It was a heck of a place.

And that sultry eve, buzzing from the Bentley, Vern Bushnell fell in love there.

It was a Tuesday so a lot of the main attractions had the night off. Just a small polka outfit and some chair dancing. Vern had guzzled a gallon of Old Style and was full of more bratwurst than Mike Ditka. After the fourth accordioned rendition of "The Blue Danube," Vern gathered his effects and headed for the door, pondering his next stop. But suddenly the atmosphere charged. His heart accelerated and his pupils dilated and the room became more vivid and three-dimensional. All before he had even set eyes on her for the first time.

The pudgy guy that owned the place came out on stage and mumbled something unintelligible in Chicagoan and pointed to the rafters where there hung a sad fabric facsimile of a chicken. The spotlight hit the chicken. The chicken yodeled. There was something supernaturally sinister yet pleasurable about the way Vern's internal organs writhed around in anticipation of the imminent unknown.

"UH OH!" shouted the proprietor. And the retired Teamsters that frequented the place got all giddy. They yelled back at him: "UH OH!"

"YOU KNOW WHAT THAT MEANS!"
"CHICKEN DANCE!!!"
"PLEASE WELCOME THE LOVELY MIA AND THE CHICKEN DANCE!"

The band played her in. And there she was. Breathtaking in her yellow leotard sparsely adorned with feathers and sparkles and sequins...

The lovely Mia.

The old Teamsters abandoned their bratwurst en masse, rushed the stage, and flapped their arms in unison, reveling in her youth and mimicking her every move as she guided them through the various sequences of the Chicken Dance.

But Vern noted not one of them. Because time had stopped for him. The polka transformed into a mesmerizing song of sirens. Mia's lithe arms wafted into the air as her exquisite fingers impersonated chicken beaks. Vern pushed through the frozen crowd and joined in her slow, sultry choreography. Their eyes locked. And as their elbows jutted into chicken wings, their souls linked.

6

A VIRGINAL, WHITE SAND BEACH

Vern and Mia shut the Heidelberg down. But this was one of those nights that wouldn't, couldn't, shouldn't end. They racked up some miles on Vern's Z-28, cruising around the perimeter of Sawnichikee, breathing the salt in the air, stealing glances at each other's moon-bathed hands and thighs and necks and hair. Their conversation flowed like the Gulf Stream.

They discovered they were star-crossed. She went to Sawnichikee High, and he'd just graduated from Riverview. There was no more bitter rivalry known to man. But just as suddenly as they had gasped at the Romeo-and-Julietness of it all, they sighed at the synchronized realization that it was a total non-issue to them both. Pheromonal insistence snuffed out high school allegiance, and the stars uncrossed.

Their conversation combusted in tandem with Tina's growling V8. Vern, coasting on amatory clouds, regaled her with spontaneously conceived plans to "just keep driving, like to the Grand Canyon or some shit!" Mia, floating on amorous jetstreams, one-upped him with double-dog-skinny-dipping-dares.

Neither was quite bold enough to call the other's bluff. But she was dazzling, and he was dazzled. He was dashing, and she was dashed. The stars looked down and sighed.

Then...

"I want to tell you something but I don't want you to get all weirded out," Vern said.

"Okay..."

"You know, back at the castle? When you were up there chicken dancing?"

"Yeah?"

Vern took a big breath. His vulnerability muscles ached from lack of exercise. He pressed through the resistance. "I had this feeling that you, well, that the world... that *everything* really, was playing a private show just for me."

"Oh yeah?"

"Yeah, like, there was a voice in my head that was smarter than me. And it was telling me where to look and what to think."

"Did you say 'a voice'?"

Mia looked at Vern with saucer eyes. His sphincter dilated.

"You think I'm nuts. Shit. I shouldn't have opened my stupid mouth—"

"No Vern no no no," Mia practically squealed. "The whole 'smarter voice talking to you' thing? *I know all about this!*"

Vern had never felt such a sudden release of tension. Not on the toilet. Not as his date manipulated his tux pants zipper in Tina's back seat after the Homecoming Dance sophomore year. Not ever.

He shuddered. "You get it? You understand?"

"Maybe you have the same thing I have," said Mia.

"What's that?"

"A divergent personality."

"A... what's that?"

Mia explained urgently, putting into words for the very first time something she had held secret in her deepest emotional cellar. "Well my parents last year found some dope in my purse and they made me go talk to this doctor who isn't actually a doctor, I don't think dad understood the letters in her degrees, I think he and mom think she's a psychiatrist or counselor but she's more like my *guru*, and she told me that I have all kinds of *wisdom*, like deep deep down, that's buried underneath a lot of other stuff that only matters right now. And that the older I get the easier it should be to get at the, uh, y'know?"

Vern nodded. His brain was baffled. But his heart and his guts, like, totally knew.

Vern's nod refueled Mia's monologue. "Anyway, for now she said to keep this to myself—but telling *you* feels so very very completely right—because my parents are super-duper-Catholic, but the guru-doctor insists that we live our lives over and over again. And each time, each life, we learn a little bit more. And she said that I'd been around a lot of times and learned a lot of stuff about the world and the Universe but that right now I'm so distracted by what's happening in this moment right here right now that I'm shutting out my old voice."

"Your smarter voice?"

"Exactly! I've sorta stuffed the old voice and all the lessons I've learned in a tunnel or something. And so there's always this argument happening between the here-and-now me and the old me. The old part of me knows exactly the right thing to do, but the other part of me can only think about what's happening right now. Like, like, like how a shark will eat your leg even if it's not hungry because your leg is right there and in front of him? Y'know? *Y'know?*"

Whether by intention or instinct, Vern had, while listening, found the turn-off to his favorite little winding sandy road that dead-ended at a tiny piece of beach surrounded by mangroves. Tina snickered to a stop like a carriage horse.

Vern turned in his seat. Took all of Mia in. Mia suddenly realized where they were. Her mouth snapped shut and she turned toward Vern. They both held their breath, as you do before moments of import.

Vern reached over and took her hand. Their fingers trembled as they intertwined.

"What's your old voice saying right now?" Vern whispered.

Mia whispered back. "Well, that's the problem. I haven't learned yet how to tell one voice from the other."

They could feel each other's hearts thudding through their palms.

"So, Vern, my whole point is... maybe you have that, too."

"A divergent personality."

Mia gulped. "Yeah. And maybe when I was dancing and everything seemed so clear to you, you were hearing your old voice. My doctor says very few people have 'em, and that most of us who do never hear 'em, much less listen to 'em."

Vern wet his lips and wound up for the pitch.

Mia began to say "I don't know why—"

But Vern kissed her before she had a chance to verbalize what she didn't know. What did she not know? Didn't matter a whit. Because all was *now*, and now was pixie dust. Now was the stars getting bigger and brighter. Now was the transcendent buzz of the universe fully audible, pounding, pulsating, FM signals coursing through their lips and tongues and teeth and saliva, through fingers fumbling and breaths halting and moans harmonizing and souls melding. Glowing bioluminescence transformed the Gulf of Mexico into a vast plane of ghosts. Elder Ones bent time and Pain Lords rent space. The cosmic timpani crescendoed.

After, their panting slowed as they lay in a sweaty heap in the back seat, limbs blissfully akimbo. They listened to the Sawnichikee night.

Vern stirred. His finger sizzled through some sweat on Mia's brow. "What's your old voice saying right now?"

She snuggled in tighter against him. "Good boy, Vern. *Gooooood* boy."

Cuter'n pigs in shit.

7

VERN FALLS OUT WITH HIS FATHER

To the casual observer, it might have seemed that Artie Bushnell was being too hard on his son, Vern. But paternally speaking Artie was not an archetypal domestic tyrant by the standards of his day. He didn't have disdain for the culture's softening of masculine ideals, nor did he feel threatened by the youth movement. But from early in his eldest son's pubescence he had been fearful that the boy might be evolving into what an Army buddy had once termed a "snarfer." The sort of guy who says things like "Ah, that's nothing!" and "Do me a favor real quick" and "Hey, smell my finger."

So the appearance of fatherly pressure was deceiving, for Artie Bushnell the pater sought only to divert the onset of his boy's full-blown snarfdom. But Vern understood this not at all. He didn't have the perspective or the vocabulary. So he subscribed to a self-pitying theory of victimization which was much more in line with what our aforementioned casual observer might hypothesize.

Basically, Vern thought his pops was an unfair, demanding bastard.

When a blissed-out Vern finally pulled Tina into the Bushnell driveway, the sun was a-risin'. Artie had been waiting up all night. His wife, Mary Ann, had lasted until three a.m. before going to bed. She'd implored her husband to abandon his watch and join her but he'd refused. In the interim between Mary Ann's retirement and Vern's homecoming, Artie drank half a bottle of Johnnie Walker Red.

The confrontation might have gone down more peaceably if both parties hadn't entered into it inebriated and from opposite ends of the emotional spectrum. Had they instead been sober and of emotion middling, it may have resulted in nothing more than a typical parent-child argument about curfews, of no historical significance. But Vern was young and empowered and drowning in the nootropic nightmare that is love, and his father was old and disenfranchised and irrelevant, and both were untethered by drink. This early-dawn encounter was pure Sophocles.

After a few predictable barbs and recriminations from both sides, the two men ripped off their shirts and mauled each other.

A loud crash from the family room roused Mary Ann and a subsequent shattering of glass roused Vern's younger brother, Bryce. Mary Ann rushed downstairs to find her husband and eldest son shirtless and snarling. Vern, performing a wheelbarrow facebuster upon Artie, was milliseconds away from bisecting the coffee table with his father's frontalis.

"VERNON!" wailed Mary Ann. "Put your father down right now!"

Bryce emerged from his bedroom just in time to see Vern abruptly dump his father on the floor. An Olan Mills portrait of the family fell off the wall. And then there was an ominous silence. Which Artie shattered by leaping to his feet, wrapping his hands around Vern's throat, and driving his son against a credenza. Thus entangled in the act of strangling his boy, Artie was unaware of his dangerous proximity to Mary Ann's rattan shelf of porcelain figurines.

"ARTIE! MY HUMMELS!"

Even amid this primeval donnybrook, Artie knew better than to endanger the Hummels. He spun Vern around and shoved him toward the sofa, sensing impending victory. But Vern, in a spry demonstration of the unfair advantages of youth, trampolined off the cushions and boomeranged toward his father. He executed a textbook tackle, shoulder into gut. They slammed to the floor, and in the ensuing mad scramble Vern ended up mounted on his father's back, pressing Artie's face into the shag carpeting.

"VERNON!" howled Mary Ann. "What are you thinking!?"

"What kind of son are you?" spat Artie.

"This kind, you old bastard!" Vern raised a clenched fist in the air and aimed it squarely at Artie's beet-red cheek.

"Mom! He's gonna kill him!" said Bryce, with a soupçon of fascinated glee.

"Vern." Mary Ann's voice was hollowed out by defeat, and this emptiness, far more awful than the screaming, finally broke through. "Let him up. Please."

Vern exhaled a gust of hot, sour wind. Artie winced. Vern lowered his fist, dismounted, and grabbed his shirt. Mary Ann rushed to Artie and helped him to his feet.

Vern turned his back and ambled toward his bedroom. All still might have been salvaged. A cooling off, a halting conversation over breakfast, a mutual mea culpa culminating in an apologetic clink of orange juice glasses. Except Artie's masculinity could not allow the confrontation to end so decidedly. Sophocles, remember? *Hamartia*. Tragic flaw.

Artie hissed, "You rotten, thankless kid. You useless bag of flesh."

Vern turned, his eyes glistening with livid, unshed tears that rightly spooked his family. Artie knew he should stop. But no. Tragedy is inevitable.

"That's right, go ahead and cry. You baby. You child. You pathetic—"

Vern heaved forward into the final catastrophic shove, and Artie was propelled helplessly backward into Mary Ann's Hummels. Tiny, porcelain, anglo heads and hands and trunks shattered into formless shards that swirled and gamboled and wafted, in seemingly never-ending slow motion, before coming to splintered rest on the floor.

Sweet Mary Ann, who'd never harmed another living soul, collapsed to her knees and wept. For her Hummels, yes. But more so for the dissolution of a world that she'd assembled sofa by rug by curtain by side table by potted fern by doily by blessed doily.

"You... You get out of this house," Artie wheezed.

"Fine by me." But Vern was frozen by the image of his mother keening on the floor.

Artie moved closer with cautious, breathless machismo.

"GET OUT!"

"I'm going!" Vern shook the dust from his feet and made his exit, slamming the front door, the echoes of which reverberated through time.

Vern revved Tina's engine, pealed out of the driveway, and roared down Ulmer Street as his father licked his wounds, his brother promoted himself to favorite son, and his mother mewled over her obliterated little friends.

Vern raced to the 7-11 on Washington Boulevard, marched to the payphone, and fed it a quarter. From his wallet, he produced the precipitous business card that had been gifted to him the previous day, though so much had happened in the interim that it seemed eons ago. The business card read:

SNEED ENTERPRISES
Sandy and Malcolm Sneed
Patriarchs

8

THE QUEEN PALM RENAISSANCE

And thence did it begin. The Sneeds had found their beagle.

Vern began his tutelage with low-impact, low-risk missions: driving the Bentley to the mechanic, mailing packages, occasionally stealing campaign signs. But he fast endeared himself to the Sneeds, with his good looks and his total lack of self-awareness, and before he knew it the Sneeds were setting him up for unwitting prestige. On the Sneed dime, Vern draped himself in Z. Cavaricci and bathed in Drakkar and turned a former crocodile farm into a pastel nightmare of a shopping center. From out of nowhere, courtesy of the Sneeds, Queen Palm had its first New Wave Real Estate Developer.

When red tape fettered the Sneeds' ambitions and their patience for pesky city ordinances began to wane, they stumbled upon Vern's true purpose in their endeavors. They ran the young pillock for City Council. Of course he won. And the last vestiges of his inbred scruples were scrubbed away.

Meantime his newfound wealth and power were catnip to Mia, who never again had to chicken dance for minimum wage plus tips. Like all 20-somethings, they thought their passion was permanent and their ascendancy pre-ordained. Mary Ann brought Bryce as her plus-one to the wedding. Vern and Artie never reconciled. The problem was, they thought they had time.

And Vern was far too busy to worry about his old man, as the Queen Palm renaissance was underway! The heart-breaking end of sweet Sawnichikee began as Vern and the Sneeds set the regal march of homogeneity into motion. The hippies handled this affront with predictable resignation and begrudgingly moved to Asheville or Costa Rica. The dear, ancient Pelican Key aristocrats died off. The drunken Lithuanian abstract expressionist retired to Long Island. The White Sox moved to Arizona. Landmarks went down, condos went up. More and more pieces of pristine public beach were privatized. The handful of locals who remained were generally far too gentle or ethical to go toe to toe with the Sneeds. And so the nostalgic bitching around town concluded more and more often with, "If you can't beat 'em..."

Even so, the magical vortex of Sawnichikee remained. In ways communal: hurricanes never made landfall there, always diverting at the last moment. Queen Palm residents, unlike the majority of coastal-dwelling Floridians, had learned not to bother investing in plywood or sandbags or backup generators.

And in ways personal: in 2011 a single mother was picking out laundry detergent at the newest Queen Palm Target store. A wave of youthful giddiness crashed over her, knocking her breath clean out and causing her to drop the Tide. She had no way of knowing that the exact spot upon which she was standing, in the laundry detergent aisle, was the very same spot where she had eaten hallucinogenic mushrooms and first kissed her teenage son's now deadbeat daddy in what was then a fertile patch of cow pasture, far from civilization.

If you'll indulge me, I also want to tell you about the joint I miss most. There was a Chinese restaurant on the main drag, The Golden Buddha. The Peking duck was atrocious, but they had a menu signed by Ernest Hemingway who stopped in for Lo Mein one day in the '50s. The building is still there. Now it's a goddamn Jimmy John's.

All to say, the Sneed's vision succeeded with such aplomb in a localized setting, they decided to go global. And Vern, their podunk figurehead, remained securely strapped to the mast. In relatively short order he hopscotched from City Councilman to State Representative, and after a couple of terms in Tallahassee to catch his breath the Sneeds catapulted him to Queen Palm's Representative in the honest-to-god United States Congress.

Which at last brings us back to the present. (If you're the sort who believes that time is linear...)

9

SEVERAL HOURS AFTER THE DEMISE
OF THE PONTUS SUPREME B-15

F riday morning Vern elected to sleep in. He felt he owed it to himself. He had won the debate the previous night, quite handily, mostly by saying nothing of substance and smiling apologetically to the camera on behalf of his unraveling opponents. Swallerman imploded at the first question about her dominatrix daughter. Schla managed maybe five coherent words, the last of which was a reverberating, un-stuttered, un-bleeped "FUCK" that would live on in glorious meme infamy. Lueke ran roughshod over all, but, as a fellow Sneed lapdog, he left Vern relatively unscathed. The others moaned and whined and awkwardly drank water in the middle of their sentences to buy time and mansplained themselves into oblivion.

So Vern returned home that night knowing he had the inside track. He was the voters' least embarrassing option. And in modern American politics, that's the sweet spot.

Things would've proceeded as they did whether he'd slept in or not, but his decision to sleep in certainly wound up the ante-conscious. That is to say, Vern slept through his opportunity to receive his bad news piecemeal, as several survivable jabs to the jaw. Vern instead received a single, concentrated, ferocious karmic uppercut.

In the night, as Vern victoriously snored unawares, fifteen miles out into the Gulf, the Sneed oil rig Pontus Supreme B-15 had pulled the old exploding act. Bubbling crude gushed with abandon, turning topaz blue waters root beer brown. The steady stream of dinosaur tonic could not be stopped in any even remotely timely fashion. When there is no emergency shut-off mechanism because such an emergency shut-off mechanism has gone up in flames along with the rest of the outfit, what does one do first? Bring in the Army Corp of Engineers or bring in one's lawyers?

By the time Vern woke up, CNN had been running aerial footage of the disaster for four hours. His cell phone torrented texts and vomited voicemails. Already the interwebs rumbled about the unseemly connection between the Sneeds' Super PAC, Vern's political success, and the zeal with which Vern had convinced the state legislature to open the Gulf for pillaging. Whoops, sorry. For "exploration."

Those who achieve great things sans merit, when confronted with large obstacles, either discover previously unknown strength and resolve or collapse when they realize they've been propped up all this time. Wanna guess how Vern responded?

Yep. He ignored his phone, reached for the whiskey, and watched himself burn on TV.

By 12:30 pm, as Vern finished his third glass of Dickel, CNN's very own Don Lemon announced that several Florida state committees, most prominently the ethics committee, planned to scrutinize Vern's various sideshows to determine whether there was any extant malfeasance. Someone would have to answer for this senseless tragedy.

One might assume that at least *some* of the attention would be on the Sneeds themselves, that it wouldn't *all* fall on Vern. But this was not the natural order, for two reasons: A) The Sneeds had a controlling interest in pretty much every media outlet in damned near every major market, and B) The way the Sneeds dealt with PR fiascoes was intentionally bland and understated, so as to bore the audience into a drooling stupor. People tend to tune in more reliably to a human trainwreck, especially when said trainwreck is reeling from a recent disaster.

Now, while it's true that Vern probably deserved what he had coming to him, it should be noted he'd never have gotten what he deserved if it didn't make for such delicious television.

10

VERN IS CONFRONTED BY THE ELKS

Pelicans hunt by dive-bombing. They stun their unsuspecting fish prey by spearing face-first into the water from on high. Vern had watched this brilliant piece of evolution from out his condo windows many a time, delighting in how the hugely jowled, gray-white birds would glide like stealth bombers just above the surface before suddenly flitting up to gain altitude. A folding of the wings and *kablamo*, plummeting beak bops obliviously swimming brain. Then simply scoop up the concussed meal.

Vern felt like that fish. He showered and shaved in a Dickel-doused daze. He didn't know what else to do but keep his appointments. All candidates get to the point where they become automatons. Somehow his tie got tied and his cuffs got linked and his driver Escalade-ferried him to his first stop of the day. His phone quivered in his pocket the entire ride, a bomb begging to go off.

The Paternal Order of Elks held their weekly meetings at the dinner theatre downtown. This often lent a dissonant motif to discussions of civic import. A somber memorial for a fallen

Elk, for example, undertaken in the mystical village of Brigadoon was only slightly less paradoxical than a presentation by Pastor Wyman on the evils of infidelity amid the garish set pieces of a British sex farce.

That particular early afternoon, Vern was set to give a speech to the Elks from the golden wheat fields of Oklahoma. He hoped against hope it might cast him in a wholesome, corn-fed light.

"I've come here today to tell you all about—"

"I HOPE YOU'RE PROUD OF YOURSELF!"

The gauntlet was thrown. Vern looked out at the ruddy old men with their plates of fried chicken, their lips glistening with animal fat and sweet tea, their gazes pulverizing his flimsy laurels.

Vern cleared his throat and tried again. Autopilot.

"To tell you all about a very exciting development for Queen Palm—"

"JUST HOW DEEP IN THE SNEEDS' POCKETS ARE YOU, YOU SELLOUT?? THE BLOOD OF THOSE RIG WORKERS IS ON YOUR HEAD!!"

The ensuing silence was the most terrifying thing Vern had ever encountered. A couple thousand years passed, or so it seemed. Then suddenly Vern's driver was at his side, whispering urgently in his ear.

"Sir, Cliff Flagler called. Says it's imperative he sees you immediately."

The mention of Flagler did it. Finally, *finally*, Vern snapped out of his self-pitying stupor. What was he doing?? He was Vern motherfucking *Bush*nell, Congressman from and soon to be Governor of the goddamn state of Florida. He had just mopped the floor last night with the best the party could throw at him. And he was gonna let a little oil spill muck all that up? No friggin' way.

Vern stood tall, lit up his megawatt apologetic smile, and said, "Gentlemen, I'm sorry, but something has come up—"

The ornery spokes-elk stood and—in a moment of rage-fueled inspiration—lifted his hands to his head, spread his fingers into an approximation of antlers, and bellowed.

"MMMWAAOOOO! MMMWAAOOOOOO!"

Vern had never heard an elk in the wild, but this one sounded furious and threatening, even if more akin to a whale climaxing.

Another elk stood, affixed finger-antlers to forehead, and bellowed. Another stood, and another. Antlers erupted at every seat and bellows echoed across the freshly painted, windswept plains of Oklahoma.

"MMWAAOOO! MMWAAOOO! *MMMWAAOOOO!!*"

Vern scampered off the stage and leaped into the back seat of his Escalade, stampede narrowly avoided.

"Get me to Flagler. Now."

11

ET TU, CLIFF FLAGLER?

E ven multi-tentacled Outer Gods can't be in two places at
once, so the Sneeds had to employ district managers in
all locations where their interests were piqued or compromised.
In Queen Palm, that honor fell to Cliff Flagler.

Flagler was an aged but eternal Lambda Chi who had
purchased a Mark VII from Vern's daddy early in the Bushnells' Sawnichikee residency. Beyond that tenuous yet insol-
uble relationship, he was also a family friend. Vern had grown
up calling him "Uncle Cliff." They went on boat rides in the
Gulf and Flagler had once helped a pre-teen Vern reel in a
snook as big as a Peugeot. Vern's family, especially Vern's
departed daddy, was about as close to Flagler's heart as the
stolid southern man's emotional accessibility would allow.

With that in mind, it was heart-rending for Flagler to be
tasked with dismantling Vern's political aspirations. While the
Sneeds had no hearts to rend, they would surely spare a
grimace for their car-washer protégé. But the Pontus Supreme
snafu needed its patsy. The hoi polloi clamored for sacrifice.

Flagler chose a little place called Raul's. He knew Vern

liked the crab croquettes and he figured that might soften the blow.

"The Elks did what?" Flagler asked.

Vern waved the question away, stuffed another deep-fried, panko-crusted crustacean in his mouth. He was famished after his 90-proof breakfast.

Flagler waited for Vern to swallow. Vern gulped his Arnold Palmer, waiting for Flagler to ring the opening bell. He was gonna come out swingin'.

Flagler dabbed the corners of his mouth with a napkin. "So."

"So?"

"I'm real proud of you, Vern. Your daddy'd be real proud, too."

Vern snorted. "You're shittin' me that's the angle you're taking."

"Hey. You had a good run at it, Vern. You did what you had to do, everyone appreciates that."

"You're talking like it's over."

"Come on, Vern. You're well-known for your steel but there comes a time when you just have to pack it in. Call it a day. You know?"

"I'm not going anywhere. I didn't do anything wrong."

"Who are you talking to here, buddy?"

"Uncle Cliff, don't do this. I need your support, for Christ's sake."

"You gotta bow out. For the good of the party. Think of the party."

"Think of the party? That's all I've been doing since day one! I've done everything right! Everything I'm told. You know that!"

Flagler glanced around. He didn't want a scene. That was another reason he'd chosen the public venue. But Vern was working himself up like a toddler into a tantrum. "Calm down there, sport."

Vern jabbed a finger. "We wouldn't even be sitting here if it weren't for me. If I hadn't thrown my weight around in oh-four —"

"Vernon. Don't you go there."

"Do you have any earthly idea how different the world would be without me? And I mean the *world*, you son of a bitch, the WORLD."

"Lower your voice, Bubba."

"I secured the state for that cheese-dick Jim Whimple. You think he ever woulda taken Florida if it hadn't-a-been for my efforts? My goddamn loyalty to the party? And now you're just gonna turn your backs on me?"

"No one's turning their backs on you, Vern. You're taking this too personally."

Vern grabbed a bottle of hot sauce and read the label. Vinegar, aged peppers, salt. He read it again. Vinegar, aged peppers, salt. It was all he could do not to melt down entirely and flip the table. Flagler sighed and tried in earnest to coax him into some semblance of calm.

"Congressman."

The honorific snapped Vern's gaze up. Flagler smiled his megawatt apologetic smile, the same one he had taught to Vern all those years ago.

"I guarantee you will be taken care of. Your loyalty will not go unrewarded."

A series of scenarios ran through Vern's head. The first few were hyper-violent. The next were more subtle, but in every one he was gloriously vindicated. He took stock of his possible advantages and approaches, put down the hot sauce bottle— which in one scenario had shattered against "Uncle Cliff's" asshole face—and overreached.

"Well how about I just call up our friend Larry King and tell him about our software guru? Huh? How about THAT?"

Flagler's smile froze and his eyes went dead cold. "That would be a very dumb thing to do."

Vern ignored the warning and kept painting himself into a corner. "I'm sure America would be interested to know what lengths we went to to get that ass-clown elected to the highest office. That would give em' something to talk about besides some stupid oil rig."

"You are being irrational."

"Am I? *Am I really??* THIS IS SO UNFAIR!"

Flagler took a calming breath. "Vern. Look, man. If it was up to me...? But it ain't. If you don't pipe down you're gonna get a whooping like you never had. You know better than anyone how frisky they can get."

Vern did know. Too well. But his incensement at that moment was so implacable that his instincts for self-preservation abandoned him and the only final fighting words he could muster were:

"Booga booga!"

Flagler signaled for the check and took out his wallet. Dropped a crisp hundred on the table. "It's gotta be what it's gotta be. Don't make a fool of yourself, buddy."

And then Cliff Flagler walked out of the place, leaving behind most of his picadillo and a supremely deflated congressman.

The waiter swung by.

"One more Arnold Palmer," Vern said. He flicked a finger at the cash. "The rest is yours."

The waiter nodded and snatched the gigantic tip before the wallowing patron could change his mind.

Vern soaked up the dregs of a bowl of black beans with a piece of Cuban bread. He felt the eyes of others on him and looked over to a table of two inveterate locals who acknowledged him with a fair measure of unguarded hostility. One wore a ratty guayabera, the other an Allman Brothers t-shirt. They were of the classic Sawnichikee stock, the line between redneck and hippie genetically muddied, their political persuasion tenuous. But their attitudes toward Vern Bushnell were apparent in their glares.

Vern gave them a friendly, man-of-the-people nod. "Gentlemen."

The man in the guayabera curled his lip. "It's about damned time you were called to the dock, man."

"Rigged a federal election, you know," said the man in the Allman Brothers t-shirt. "Oh, sure. And that's just the tip of it."

In his younger days, Vern would've vehemently defended himself with swear words and demeaning rebuttals, but he'd learned better in the ensuing years to employ honey whenever possible.

"I am always pleased to engage personally with my constituents," he said, "but I've really had a hell of a day."

"*You've* had a hell of day? What about your so-called constituents?" barked guayabera. He lifted his plate aloft. "This is probably the last plate of Gulf grouper I'll ever be able to eat! You and your goddamn son-of-a-bitchin' drilling."

"Energy policy is a very complex issue," said Vern.

"You value nothing, is the problem!"

Vern's autopilot hiccuped. "Values are very important, yes."

"When I was a kid," said the Allman Brothers tee, "you could pull oysters right out of the bay and eat 'em."

Vern had no response to this culinary nostalgia. He sat in silence. The Arnold Palmer appeared. He held it up and toasted the two men. They saluted back with middle fingers. Then his driver once again hustled in to rescue him with ear whispers.

Vern's heart somehow simultaneously dropped to his gut and leaped to his throat. "What do you mean?"

Whisper whisper.

"How many of 'em??"

Whisper whisper whisper.

"Jesus. Did somebody call the police?"

Whisper.

"Well someone should just call the police. Let's get over there now."

The driver marched out dialing 911. Vern followed, weaving through tables, but his automation was not yet fully short-circuited. Without thinking, he stopped and turned back to his constituents. "You enjoy your meal, gentlemen."

"Bite me," said guayabera through a mouth of masticated grouper.

12

THE AZURE TIDES

Queen Palm, née Sawnichickee, all nostalgia and romanticism aside, had never been utopian. There had always been shady drifters and horse thieves and con artists in tow with every annual migration of tin-can tourists. Civically speaking, there had always existed an excess of corruption in the City Hall area. This was harmless, local vice. By and large, inconsequential.

But as we've seen, the Sneeds were not ones to keep anything localized. And they certainly weren't about to stomach such frivolous waste of acreage (orange groves on million-dollar lots?!) or such underutilized lack of oversight by the city's departments; with such a Dixiecratic demographic of small-time politicians and such a pliable populace of blissfully unaware citizens, great things could be accomplished.

Galaxy Burger, between 1962 and 1985, had purchased grade-A ground round beef from Tom Muff's Butcher Shop. Galaxy's own Hunter Hurley would form the beef into patties and put them on wax paper and stick them in the cooler where they would wait to be layed out on a hot griddle by Ray

Freeman Jr., whose mastery as a short-order cook was unmatched. Hunter and Ray and Tom Muff the butcher, this noble triumvirate, brought burgers to the good folks of Sawnichickee every day of the year except Sundays, Christmas, Thanksgiving, Easter, and two weeks in June when Hunter would visit his folks in Buffalo.

In 1984 the Sneed Brothers bought the property that Galaxy Burger had leased for almost a quarter-century. They shelled out more than the entire lease would cost for the next ten years. Astronomical funds to you and me. To them, a pittance. They jacked the rent, no negotiation. Hunter sadly retired; he could've started over, as the name "Galaxy Burger" still carried cachet, but his spirit was broken. I think he ended up in Buffalo after inheriting his parents' house. Ray took his griddle skills to a tiki bar up the key. Meantime the Sneeds demolished Galaxy Burger just short of its 25th anniversary and brought in a franchise that bought their beef, frozen and already formed into patties, from a national supplier.

This was a loss for Tom Muff the butcher, but it didn't mean total ruin. Tom Muff hung in there owing to a loyal clientele of housewives and an Italian restaurant. Then the Sneeds turned the old newspaper building into a supermarket that also bought from a national supplier, in bulk, so was able to offer a less expensive albeit genetically modified alternative to Tom Muff's Butcher Shop. Tom's natural charm and blood-stained smock couldn't compete with the windfall of coupons and bogos. The housewives abandoned him en masse, with apologies on their lips and savings in their pocketbooks.

The Sneeds were on a roll.

The Sawnichickee Historical Society, bless their hearts, did what they could to stop the rezoning of the old Toolwood District, but even their shrill chanting could not compete with seemingly endless capital. And who could blame the city commission for essentially acknowledging the rightwiseness of the Free Market?

Exacerbating the problem was the fact that the city commissioners were aging and, in many cases, kind of kooky. They were effortlessly convinced by the new arrivals that beach bonfires and public intoxication were distasteful and promptly passed an ordinance against the consumption of alcoholic beverages on the beach. This extended to any new dining establishments wanting to take advantage of the sand and sunsets. There was but one grandfathered hold-out the summer before the oil spill. The Azure Tides stood proudly, as it had since 1947, the lone toe-hold for the last scrappy vestiges of Old Florida charm along the water. It was dimly lit and decorated with lanterns and fishing nets.

At the risk of sounding like a class warrior, I must interject at this point that there was a time when people of modest means, and in many cases less than modest means, could find themselves living blissfully close to or even on the Gulf of Mexico. The Azure Tides was made for those times.

By last summer those times were such a distant memory that even I, who swung through often, could only really think of them as a fleeting ideal rather than an actual reality. The shores, where once the sun and the sand and a cooler of beer were the only fixtures, now provided tenuous foundation to condominiums, private beach clubs, and a laughable stretch of public beach where anything remotely kinetic or joyful was, if not strictly prohibited, at the very least distinctly frowned upon.

Through no fault of its own, the Azure Tides had become a curiosity more than a landmark. A place less for revelry than irony. Surrounded on either side by a garish collection of newly constructed giant gazebos and hot tubs overflowing with

Chateauneuf-du-Pape, the rickety, rustic Azure Tides managed to stay afloat.

Then a series of unfortunate yet entirely predictable events dominoed the Azure Tides toward destruction. First, the winter people's complaints about the noise reached their crescendo, and an ordinance passed banning any live music after 9 p.m. A hell of a blow, but the Azure Tides survived.

Then the winter people began to complain about the aesthetic nature of the place and offered to have it painted. The regulars scoffed. The ancient proprietor, Mickey Knox, didn't even open the letter from the condo association with its colors samples and list of local painters. The Azure Tides endured.

Then the winter people began to call the cops if even one extra chorus of "Margaritaville" or "No Woman No Cry" echoed past 9:01 pm. Then the winter people, whose need for private parking had been steadily eating up the open spaces of grass and gravel, began having cars towed. This was getting dangerously personal, closer and closer to foul play. Yet still the Azure Tides trudged on, whipped and battered for sure, but nursing its buzz and applauding for the spectacular sunsets every night.

But then, finally, Mickey Knox's soul went out with the tide and didn't come back. The winter people made half-assed attempts at public mourning but privately popped the Dom Perignon. And the realtor that Mickey's kids brought in was a good friend of Vern's and Vern was looking to open a Waldorf Astoria and so the pieces came together very smoothly.

And on this particular day, the day after Vern won the debate and the Pontus Supreme exploded and the day the Elks bellowed and Cliff Flagler sprang for crab cakes—can you believe it?—the Azure Tides was set for demolition.

When Vern's Escalade pulled up to the Azure Tides a daisy chain of granola people and parrotheads had formed around the ramshackle shanty. Rotting and hurricane-beaten, it contrasted sharply with the sparkling white condominium buildings on either side.

Vern noted the demolition equipment in limbo and the workers, inactive and on-the-clock, waiting for this PR nightmare to subside so they could begin their work. The foreman approached and knocked on the tinted window. Vern lowered the window halfway.

"What's the problem, Bobby?"

"Well, these folks are awful pissed off, sir."

"Look at the damned thing. It won't last another tropical storm. I did those old folks a favor taking it off their hands."

"Sure. But all the same, they seem pretty attached to it. You know?"

A middle-aged cracker in a Flora-Bama tank-top approached the Escalade with a protest sign in one hand and a Miller Lite in the other.

"Hemingway drank here, you capitalist pig!" he howled.

Vern smiled automatically, but his reaction times were slowing. He bit back a snarl and said, "Hemingway drank everywhere, sir. We can't let that stand in the way of progress." The man weakly kicked Vern's front tire and rejoined the other protestors.

"OK, Bobby. Here's what we're gonna do. I'm gonna send a patrol car by to drive around the block a few times, you know, all menacing like. If they all run away, you proceed. If not, send your boys home and we'll see where we are tomorrow."

"That'll do."

Bobby ambled back to his crew.

13

TRAFFIC ON THE ROAD TO AMELIORATION

Given the events of the day, the Azure Tides was of tertiary concern to Vern. Financially consequential, for sure, if not as directly connected to his political survival. But still, the protestors and the delay and the sheer pathetic *nuisance* of it all added to the growing throb behind his eyes. Vern massaged his temples.

The driver finished the SOS to the local precinct and lowered his phone. "Where to, sir?"

"Gimme a sec, Driver, just gimme a sec," Vern mumbled.

By the by, this entirely competent driver's name was Harrison, though I'm not sure if that's first or last. Harrison had taken "Stand-Up Boot Camp" at the local comedy club half a dozen times, and when duty to the Congressman didn't call he hit every open mic within two hundred miles. None of this mattered to Vern, though, who had asked and forgotten Harrison's name so often that both men had silently agreed to simply use "Driver." But I thought you should know.

Vern tapped on the headrest. Driver looked up from his

phone. He'd been texting himself the perfect punchline to a joke he'd been chewing on for days.

"Sir?"

"Home, Driver. I need to check on Mia, change my shirt, I've sweated through. Gotta figure out my next move."

"Very good, sir."

But, of course, traffic was not moving on the causeway. Not even local titans can escape gridlock on the causeway. Time ticked by, relentless. Vern could feel Flagler and the Sneeds, plotting his doom. What to do? Request an audience? Enter on knees, hat in hand? Apologize? Fall on his sword? Take one for the team?

Or follow through on his threat?

Or, HEY, what about this? Find another fall guy? But who, who, who who who?

Vern pulled out a hanky and wiped his forehead. The traffic basked in the sun. Its Apollonic heat was augmented by passage through an unsightly smog that had grown increasingly visible over the past decade. Even the state-of-the-art A/C in Vern's Escalade couldn't compete with the oppressive torridity.

"Driver."

"Sir?"

"Any more air?"

"Already at max."

"Then how about the radio?"

"You got it."

Driver clicked on the radio, and the traffic magically picked up a few mph. Vern half-listened as he took in the evolving vista: countless cranes dotting the burgeoning skyline, towering only slightly above the skeletal frames of what would be garish residential monuments to a new brand of gauzy opulence. It was geometrically elegant or horrifyingly hellscapish, depending on your level of equity.

"And if you ask ME, Vern Bushnell is a HERO."

Vern perked up. The talk-radio narrative had zeroed in on him. An uffish, coked-up pundit who also owed his career to the Sneeds was coming to Vern's defense.

"And I'll tell you why. He is resolute. I don't think I'm too out of line saying that the vast majority of our elected representatives, even in our own party, are so damned wishy-washy. But Vern Bushnell doesn't allow himself to disassociate from his principles over a lot of 'what-ifs'..."

Stunning poetry to Vern's ears.

"...and to have that kind of backbone in this sort of environment, well, they can call it malfeasance all they want but I challenge them to explain to me how adherence to an infallible set of principles suddenly became malfeasance."

And just like that, the throbbing in Vern's head evaporated. He *was* resolute. No other fall guy. No crying a boon. He didn't need the party. Or the Sneeds. *They* needed *him*.

14

A PORTRAIT OF MIA

I t wouldn't be accurate to call Mia a "bird in a gilded cage." It would be esoteric and misleading. On many levels. (And from a literary perspective it would also be an unforgivably hackneyed shortcut.)

It would be misleading because it would suggest that (A) Mia was some sort of enchanted songstress being held against her will, and (B) the cage in which she was held, metaphorically or not, was 'gilded', which wasn't the case. But (A) Mia was not a bird lacking agency. She'd made her own decisions, by and large. And (B) Vern's condominium building was a graceless, granite obelisk with windows. It jutted into the sky from between two miraculously preserved Spanish Revival commercial buildings. Vern and Mia lived on the eighth floor in a suite laid out especially for them by the architect, for whom Vern had finagled the contract. It had all the modern trappings but you'd never mistake it for "gilded."

These distinctions would move a conscientious scribbler to try to find some other vivid and relatively concise means to convey that Mia possessed a beautiful spirit that had found itself confined.

So try this on. As Vern's hubris grew, Mia became adept at shushing her smarter voice. It wasn't easy. When her will alone proved unable to silent the shrieked warnings of her older, wiser self, she brought in the heavy guns. Narcotics provided blessed calm. Thus her conviviality, so waxing full all those years ago on stage and in the moonlight, had waned far past gibbous to its last clinging sliver of crescent.

Even filtered through the Dilaudid, the images on the news that morning had cut her self-concept to the quick. All those souls, drenched in flame and sea. And how had Vern reacted? She watched him watching the images looped on the news, with that pathetic pitying look on his face, drinking and drinking, unable or unwilling to just stand up, this racketeer, this enemy of the people... Mia realized with sudden crystalline clarity that she and he were both far gone.

Ah well, hiccup and la de da.

After Vern left for his lunch and his whatever else he spent his days doing, Mia plopped down on the couch with two bottles, gin and pills. She changed the channel and tried to drown the last desperate gasps of her smarter voice.

Hours passed. Medicated inebriation set in. QVC blathered. The door banged open. She shifted her eyeballs—god DAMN they were heavy—and even though she knew it was Vern, god DAMN it looked like Robert Mitchum.

She raspberried her lips. "The spineless bastard couldn't tell me himself? He had to send you?"

"Ah, Jesus." Vern snatched up the pill bottle, shook it like a baby's rattle. "How many of these things did you take?"

Not enough to kill her—she was spineless, too, in her way— but enough to sell the hallucination that her husband had sent Robert Mitchum as an emotional stunt double. As Robert-Vern confiscated her Bombay Sapphire she admired his masculine jawline and commanding eyes.

"I might have gone for James Garner, but Mitchum is a heady choice."

"Dollbaby, what are you...?"

He noticed the muted flatscreen. QVC with closed captioning. The product being peddled was an outdoor shower for pets.

Vern squinted. "The hell is that thing?"

Mia said nothing.

"What's wrong with the dang hose?"

"I don't know, but you were great in *Thunder Road*."

Vern wondered to himself what had ever brought them together. Then, for a split second, he remembered. The Chicken Dance. The early nights on the beach. Tina the Z-28. Hazy memories of an altogether different girl and boy. Then, a tubby Boston Terrier indiscreetly writhed around in the pet shower. He snapped back to. Things to do.

"Did Rosa pick up my suits?"

"You know what I'm gonna Netflix later? *The Electric Horseman*. No, wait, shit, that's Robert *Redford*, ugh."

Vern opened the fireproof safe secreted in the back of the pantry and pulled out a small black book. This book was full of phone numbers and addresses and PINs and verification codes that he'd been carefully instructed never ever to store electronically. He slipped it in his pocket. Ammunition.

"Mia?"

"Robert?"

Vern exhaled hard, counted to ten. "Did Rosa pick up my suits?"

"I don't know nuthin' about any suuuuits."

Vern went into the bedroom, dug around in his walk-in closet, came back out with a duffle bag and a dry-cleaner-fresh suit. He also had a clean shirt. He started changing in front of her as QVC hawked an LED light you put in your toilet.

"Oooooh, Robert, look! Let's get a GloBowl. It's a nightlight for when you have to pee."

Vern mashed the cuff buttons closed. "This lifestyle of yours, Mia... It's not healthy. You have to get some sun. For the Vitamin D. You should open a window."

A saleswoman flipped on the GloBowl and demo'd with a child's water pistol. Mia cackled. "Looks like the fountain at the Bellagio!"

Vern stomped to the window and yanked open the shades revealing their Gulf view. Though the vista was hazy with smog and natural gas vapors and the water was likely toxic, it was quite a stunning view.

Mia moaned and covered her eyes.

"Mia. I've got some stuff I've gotta do. I'm not sure I'll be home tonight. I want you to promise me that you'll remember to eat. Can you make me that promise?"

The sun pounded against the glass, like someone locked in a closet begging to be let out. Mia turned her suddenly lucid gaze to her sad, sad husband. No more Mitchum.

"Why'd you do it, Vern?"

He blinked. But forged on. "I don't mean to lecture you, but if you're gonna be drinking as much as you are, you just gotta eat. And cut the pills."

"You didn't do all this for me, did you?"

"Honey, would you please—

"I could've done with a lot less."

"Just a sandwich now and then. Please. For me."

"Maybe you could just... drop me back off where you found me?"

Vern looked down at her, crumpled and bathrobed, and had his own moment of crystalline clarity. In super fast-forward, he saw a replay of his complete abandonment of the life they'd planned. But caught up as he was in the frantic scramble to salvage his own ambitions, he drew back from the cliff's edge of acknowledging his complicity. Mia's fate—slowly losing her mind in an eight-floor condo—was a bed she had made. He hadn't condemned her to sleep in it. That was on her. Now, had he pulled back the covers, brought her a glass of warm milk, fluffed the pillow, even tucked her in a little? Maaaybe. And he'd reflect on that. Later. Just, you know, not right now.

Even so, he gently pushed a couple strands of sweaty hair from her forehead. Thumb-wiped a dribble of drool from the corner of her mouth.

"I'll be back as soon as I can."

She pulled away from his touch. "Sure. Whatever you say."

He shouldered the duffle, grabbed the suit, and left. In the elevator, he patted the black book in his pocket. The talk-radio host's words still fired his blood. The image of his hollowed-out wife froze his heart. As soon as he handled the Sneeds, he'd find some way to make it right with Mia.

15

VERN ENABLES THE FOURTH ESTATE

Between Vern's ascent to and descent from his lair that day, a representative of the press had been tipped off to his whereabouts and laid in wait outside his building. As he emerged from the front entrance an amped-up lady in a periwinkle pantsuit charged at him with a microphone extended like a lance. "Congressman Bushnell! Congressman Bushnell!" A beleaguered dude with a camera and backward ballcap huffed to keep up.

Vern suppressed his initial impulse to sprint for the Escalade. He squinted at her. Opportunity? Kismet? How to play, how to play...

"Congressman Bushnell. Gail Hite. ABC-7."

"Sure, of course. Hi there, Gail," he said, waving at Driver to wait a sec.

"How do you respond to the suggestions that you are, in some way, to blame for today's tragedy?"

"Hm?" The black book *thump-thumped* in his pocket.

"Congressman, are you to blame??"

Old habits die hard. Interview Jujitsu 101: *Deflection.* "Well, Gail, I'd have to say that's pretty silly."

"Silly?"

"I mean, how would... I mean, what did... what did I do? Did I build the rig? Did I write the checks? There are several parties involved, blame in these situations is never cut'n'dried. Tapping a fall guy is just lazy on your part, I must say."

A breeze gusted. Gail's hair was as implacable as her questioning. "But you can't deny that your policies and your platforms could be reasonably linked to entities that in fact financed your—"

Interview Jujitsu 201: *Embrace Victimhood.*

"Gail, this is a witch hunt. It's all misdirection."

"Meaning that you deny any—"

Quick pivot into 301: *Good ol' boy/humble origins.* "Gail, listen to me. This is my home. I was born here. I grew up here. My daddy sold cars and my momma raised my brother and me herself. I met my wife here. Right here in Queen Palm. I've been here since it was called Sawnichickee, for goodness' sake. Do you think I would ever do anything to—"

Thump-thump went the black book against his thigh. *Woosh* went the Gulf breeze. The hazy curtain dividing past from present fluttered open. Vern inhaled the salty air and nostalgia inflated his lungs. He held his breath and realized that Gail Hite of ABC-7 was absolutely right. My god what he wouldn't give to watch the fiddler crabs scurry and eat coquina soup and sail the afternoon away on a bright yellow Hobie Cat. And what about reptile farms, orange stands, honey sticks, Stuckey's, the used book store where he sold his dog-eared comic books, fucking lightning bugs! There used to be lightning bugs! The nostalgia was overwhelming. He even felt nostalgic for things he had never known personally or experienced in real-time. Ghosts stirred. The garish monuments to "development" up and down the Gulf's shore suddenly emitted a penumbra of much humbler structures with much nobler foundations. Human experience covered over by human experience covered over by human experience, like rings in a tree trunk or layers of paint on an old wooden fence. This land, this place where water and sand pushed and pulled, wasn't just a collection of memories. It was an actual physical location, composed of matter and atoms, whose existence had been revoked forevermore, owing partially to the natural ravages of time, sure, but expedited adroitly by the aimless and ill-considered ambition of Vern and others of his ilk.

Oh yes. He was responsible. But so were many others.

"Congressman Bushnell?"

He exhaled the past. Re-found his grip on the present. Put a swift and determined kibosh on laments and recriminations, considered how he might best find the name of action.

"Gail, let me just say this. I played my part, yes. And I will take full responsibility for my actions. But that's not enough. There's a whole gang of folks, higher-up folks who—"

"Higher up? But you are running for *Governor*, how much higher can you get?"

"Gail, I don't mean to belittle the intelligence of the general public, not at all, but the bulk of y'all just can't fathom—"

Vern noted Gail's eyes widening. Her reporter's spidey sense was all a-tingle. Rightfully so. Vern adjusted so that the camera-dude would get his good side, then fired his warning shot across the Sneeds' bow.

"I could tell you some things, Gail, but most of y'all would just say 'huh?' Again, not to belittle you, but you don't have all the facts. I have them. I know them. And these folks have their tracks pretty well covered so no one could expect you to know, but I've got the hard proof."

Vern's bloodstream flooded with adrenaline. Gail Hite of

ABC-7 also realized that a threshold had been breached and she was momentarily daunted by the weight of the journalistic gift she'd just been given. Then she went giddy with the prospect of award-worthy scoopage. They looked at each other for a wordless beat.

"Congressman. Are you suggesting... a *conspiracy?*"

He gestured to Driver. The Escalade eased up. He smiled his megawatt apology smile. Employed one last bit of Interview Jujitsu. 401: *Always leave 'em wanting more.* "I think I'm done talking to you for now. But call my office later. I'll tell you things that'll curl your toes. Thank you and God bless."

16

VERN'S FATE IS SEALED BY TWO
ANCIENT REPTILES

The Sneeds weren't ones to put all their eggs in one orange crate. They had their fingers in the civic atmosphere of localities far and wide. This is not to say they were beyond having scruples. They didn't interfere aimlessly. They set their sights and vast resources on a given community only if its local issues could be of benefit or detriment to Sneeds, Inc.

Nashville was an excellent example. Nashville was, and remains, a fine, fine city. It has a long history of sturdy, decent, pragmatic people of great skill and ingenuity. Some of the most beautiful sounds ever emitted for the human ear originated in Nashville. It was and is a city to revere and a city worth saving. About the time the Sneeds began to feed off of Nashville, it had a six-point-seven percent unemployment rate. Six-point-seven is not a large number, but six-point-seven percent of 601,222 isn't a tiny number.

Now, there was talk of a rapid transportation system in Nashville. Any given Nashvillian with no access to an automobile due to being down on their luck would now be able to expand their job searches by a radius of twenty miles or more. To the favor of the gainfully employed, it would ease traffic and congestion and cut commute times significantly. And for the world at large, the significant lowering of carbon consumption in Nashville and the subsequent easement of emissions would be a small but meaningful step toward stemming the aggressively rising sea levels.

The problem with this unicorn-and-rainbow notion was that if it was as successful as its proponents predicted, there would be fewer people driving cars and purchasing gasoline. The Sneeds owned a shit-ton of shares in Lafayette Oil and Energy, and Lafayette Oil and Energy had established itself quite handily in Nashville with ever-multiplying outposts of its affiliate, Froggie's Gasoline, Tobacco, and Food Store.

So the Sneeds took a Santa bag of money and shelled the town with "helpful information" about the threat of certain tragedy at the hands of government overreach. Fliers, pamphlets, newspaper and television ads, "rallies" with free hamburgers, all sponsored by the Friends of James Madison, an allegedly grassroots political action committee founded and relentlessly funded by the Sneeds.

Nashville's rapid transit solution was a noble project strangled in infancy by the invisible hand.

Similar defeats befell a food co-op in Charleston, a high school arts program in Newport News, a shelter for abused women in Jacksonville, and the Columbus Zoo. Just how organic produce, a teen improv troupe, sheltering victims, and feeding giraffes would stand in the way of the Sneeds turning profit I don't pretend to understand. But, again, I want to be clear: there was no malice or tenuously motivated evil at play in any of these cases. It was just business, and the Sneeds had the profound advantage of possessing wholly reptilian hearts. A sense of humanity is very, very costly.

Cliff Flagler had just enough humanity left to cause profound inner debate as he reported to the Sneeds. Vern was like a son, but based on that brief lunch meeting, he was losing his bearings. If he were to descend into some sort of "awakening" and blow up, the shrapnel could take out a lot of good men. Flagler couldn't allow that to happen. He was, after all, a steward of civic propriety.

He sat in a plush chair, facing the Sneeds, who sat at opulent, matching desks, side by side. The entire wall behind them was a window looking out on the gator-filled pond on their estate. To Cliff's left was a fireplace he could stand in without ducking. To his right loomed a bank of monitors and flatscreens that flickered with every news channel and market tracker, though one screen defiantly played classic Looney Tunes.

Flagler watched the brothers eat pulled pork sandwiches. They ate like strange animals. Prim like raccoons with their tiny little washing hands, but simultaneously bestial like a gator lunging and rolling you to death underwater. He was hesitant to address them until they'd finished eating, but when Sandy paused briefly mid-chew and looked to Flagler impatiently, Flagler spoke.

"Vern's coming loose. If we're not careful, he may go off the deep end."

"What do you mean, off the deep end?" Glistening barbeque sauce dotted Sandy's lips.

Flagler couldn't watch directly. Their synchronized chewing made him queasy. He spoke toward the ceiling. "Well, he's not taking it all very well. In his view, you know, he took a lot of risks for you, and he feels very strongly that you are maybe not showing him... well, this whole business with the spill and all? He feels that he's taking a sizable fall and you're offering little in the way of gratitude."

"Gratitude??" Malcolm sneered, his voice dripping with disdain and pig fat. As far as Malcolm Sneed was concerned, gratitude was a luxury only the poor could afford.

Flagler decided to clean his glasses for as long as the brothers kept eating. Eyes down, eyes down. "So, he's hinting that he might speak out publicly on any number of matters which, of course, we have plenty of complimentary angles to give the public. But, all the same, it is disconcerting."

Sandy wiped his mouth with a square of monogrammed linen that cost more than the average citizen's weekly grocery bill. "Please stop talking."

"Yes sir."

"What I've managed to gather from your rambling is that our Vern Bushnell is feeling down and out because we're not taking full credit for an oil spill and is, therefore, threatening to air our dirty laundry."

"He's weak," Malcolm sneered again. "He might scare you, Cliff, but he'd never have the balls to go public."

"Sir, with all due respect, you didn't see him. He feels cornered. Trapped. And that's when—"

"Shut it." Malcolm was working himself up. "Little pissant talks about *gratitude*. Then threatens us? That's *gratitude*? Where's HIS gratitude? I never liked the kid, myself."

Sandy cleared his throat. Malcolm growled but came to heel, snarfed another bite.

"Cliff." Sandy's voice was unnervingly calm.

"Sir?"

"What does he know? Does he know a lot?"

"He does, sir. A lot."

"A LOT a lot?"

"The whole shebang."

"Mmmmm." Sandy took a sip of sparkling water, steepled his fingers. "Does he have documentation?"

Flagler nodded. "Yes sir. We trained him well. Nothing digital. But he's got his little black book. Real leather. His name's embossed. I got it for him as a gift when—"

"Are we going to have to kill him?"

Flagler's face collapsed.

"Sir?"

"I'm joking, Cliff."

"Oh. Oh, yes, of course, sir," said Flagler. Then he mustered a chuckle.

"We appreciate you looking out," Sandy said. "It's not a problem. Bushnell is not a problem."

To add assurance, Malcolm said, "Happens all the time." *Snarf.*

Sandy nodded sagely. "We'll talk him down, Cliff. Rest easy."

Flagler exhaled audibly.

"Thank you. Thank you, sir. Sirs. Thank you."

Just then the butler oozed into the room. He aimed a remote control at one ginormous flatscreen and pushed a button. The afternoon news splashed across the monitor.

"I thought you should know, Master Sneed."

The butler disappeared as the voice of Vern Bushnell—speak of the devil!—emanated from the TV.

"Gail, I don't mean to belittle the intelligence of the general public, not at all, but the bulk of y'all just can't fathom—"

"Oh shit oh god oh no," Flagler spluttered.

"And these folks have their tracks pretty well covered so no one could expect you to know, but I've got the hard proof."

"Oh, Vern, goddammit." Flagler pulled out his phone.

"Leave it be," Sandy hissed.

"Congressman. Are you suggesting... a conspiracy?"

Sandy muted Gail Hite of ABC-7's breathless outro.

Digestive gasses worked their way up Malcolm's windpipe

and exited his mouth in a death-rattley burp that formed words. "So we ARE going to have to kill him."

Flagler mustered another chuckle, but this time there was no wink-wink-nudge-nudge.

"Cliff! Call Bill Snowden," Malcolm said.

Flagler's eyes popped out of his head. "Sn-sn-snowden??"

Sandy shook his head. "Calm down, Malcolm."

"This needs to be taken care of tonight!"

"We can't kill him. Not yet."

"The kid is gonna put on a show if we don't act quickly."

"Vern, entirely through dumb luck, unfortunately has made himself indispensable. Cliff, would you please?"

Flagler pulled his eyes back into their sockets and then rattled off all the ins and outs that only Vern knew. All the valuable and volatile information. Taken separately? Shrug. A collection of anecdotes, each easily explained and excused. But taken collectively? Shudder. A damning oral history of the twisted past decade in Florida politics. Flagler spoke for a while. Long enough that the TV news replayed Gail Hite's encounter with Vern two more times.

Sandy clucked sadly. "Pity all of that exists in the tormented head of an unraveling man. Cliff, my apologies about before. You were right. We must act carefully."

"At least until we get our hands on his book and pump everything useful out of him," Malcolm said. "So what do we do? We either keep him as the candidate, blow our whole wad on a lost cause just so he doesn't feel unappreciated." *Sneersnarf.* Speaking while chewing. "Or we watch him go on Rachel Maddow and prepare ourselves for federal indictments."

"There is a third possibility," purred Sandy Sneed.

"Hmmm?"

Sandy glanced at Flagler. Weighed the need to know. Spoke sorta kinda outta the corner of his mouth.

"The... the *Project*."

Malcolm cocked his head. "The Project?"

Sandy sighed. Malcolm cocked his head the other way. Flagler stayed quiet and made himself as small as he could.

The penny dropped. Malcolm's face lit up. "Oh! The Project!"

The two brothers stared at each other, communicating via mind-meld. To Flagler, it looked like they were about to kiss.

"Cliff," Malcolm said, not breaking eye contact with his brother. "Call Vern. Summon him—"

"Perhaps we should use the word 'invite' instead?" Sandy interjected.

"Ah yes. That's good. Call Vern and tell him we are inviting him to a sit-down—"

"—a dinner—"

"A dinner. At our new country club."

"Yes. The Orlando club. Offer the Gulfstream. Private charter. Red carpet."

Malcolm nodded. "Lure him to the airport."

Sandy nodded in unison. "Snatch before he boards."

The brothers stared at each other. Flagler held his breath. The brothers turned their anaconda gazes onto him. He got the picture and exited backward, bowing like a royal subject. He sat trembling in his car for a few moments. Whatever this "Project" was, Flagler didn't want to know. He had the thought that perhaps the brutal abruptness of Snowden would have been a mercy.

Flagler shoved that thought aside and called Vern.

17

VERN VISITS HIS MOTHER

Gail Hite had wrapped as Vern zoomed away in the Escalade. She waited a whole five seconds before taking him up on his offer to call his office and schedule her exclusive. She actually didn't wait, but it did take her five seconds to fumble out her phone and find the correct number.

Vern got the text from his office. Interview with Gail tomorrow, special coverage directly after the 5 pm news. Live. Teasers were already running on every commercial break. They were even going to pre-empt *Wheel of Fortune*. Vern Bushnell was bumping *Wheel of Fortune*!

The *Wheel* news more than anything snapped Vern into a heightened state of awareness. This was happening. He was doing this. Tomorrow, absolutely everything would change.

He found himself in desperate need of seeing his mommy.

"Driver. Flower shop. Then a quick drop-in on Mary Ann and Bryce."

"You got it."

Poor Bryce. If Vern and Bryce had been twins, Vern would've strangled his brother with his umbilical cord. Fortunately for Bryce, he had been born a blessed two years after Vern. While this spared Bryce the humiliating experience of prenatal death, it didn't lead him to a carefree life. Because his older brother was out there. And he was bigger and stronger.

Vern never attempted to literally end Bryce's life at any point. In truth, he was sincerely fond. But it could be put forth by an armchair behaviorist that this sibling rivalry was laced with a skosh more sadism than might be healthy.

Growing up, Vern would often break into the bathroom while Bryce was having a movement and dangle a lizard over his head. With no clean or clear means of escape, Bryce could only whimper. Well into adulthood Bryce still had cautious bowels: only in his mother's house or his own apartment, with the door locked, all corners and crannies checked for geckos, the sink running, and a scented candle lit. This was but one symptom of his chronic fastidiousness which intensified with every passing year.

Vern would advise Bryce, with brotherly concern as a front, that if he didn't lose weight by the time he was twelve he'd be fat forever. He got a sick thrill out of watching his perfectly healthy and adorably tubby little seven-year-old brother jogging in determined circles around the backyard. It was also a benefit to Vern when Bryce insisted on eating nothing but carrots, which yielded Vern vegetable easement and a bounty of delicious, buttery starch all for himself. Even after he turned twelve and clocked in at a bony seventy-two pounds, Bryce remained compulsively obsessive about his diet and exercise regimen. The result of Vern continually and maliciously moving the goalposts.

Now Bryce's khaki suit draped itself over his anemic frame like a three-piece tunic. His voice creaked timidly from behind his epiglottis.

"Nice of you to stop by."

This was as bold as Bryce got.

Vern shouldered through the front door, knocking his wisp of a brother aside. "How is she?" He found some orange juice in the refrigerator and proceeded to drink it directly from the jug.

"Mama's taken to calling out for her childhood dog. Yumyum. Remember she told us about him? Died when she was nine. She's been calling out for him all morning."

"Weird."

"The Doctor said that her confusion could be the result of a UTI."

Vern echoed phonetically. "Uh-tee?"

"You, tee, eye, Vern."

Vern shook his head and chugged more juice.

"Are you going to make me say the whole thing? UTI." Bryce looked around embarrassed and his voice dropped to muttering. "Urinary Tract Infection. God."

Vern chuckled. Of course he knew what a UTI was. Bryce's face turned that hilarious red color that meant Vern had got to him.

"Gotcha."

"*Veeeeern.*"

"When you gonna get wise, Bee-rice?"

Brothers are the same everywhere.

Vern put the juice back in the fridge. He had never given much thought to his mother's urinary tract and he'd certainly never heard of any connection between a woman's urinary tract and sporadic spells of delirium. It almost made him angry that such an innocuous malady could cause a sturdy, sober, educated woman to forget what year it was or start calling for her childhood dog.

"Is she awake?"

Bryce nodded and led him into their mother's bedroom.

Mary Ann Bushnell sat on the edge of her bed. Vern was taken aback by how frail she'd gotten since last he'd dropped by three, four weeks ago. Sad tufts of white hair stuck out from underneath her auburn wig. For a moment it seemed he could see straight through her.

"Mama, it's Vern."

She didn't stir.

"Can you hear me, mama?"

Bryce huffed. "She can hear you, Vern. She's not deaf."

"I brought you an orchid, Mama. A white one."

Met with silence, Vern placed the orchid on the dresser and picked up a family photo on the dresser. The photographer had gotten lucky and captured the four of them all smiling at the same moment. They looked like a genuinely loving unit. Just before this moment, pubescent Vern had been pretending innocence for a perfectly aimed wet willy as Bryce wailed and pawed at the saliva coating his ear. Just after the click-flash, Vern's eyes had brimmed with tears he refused to shed from the perfectly aimed whack on the back of his head doled out by dear, departed Artie. Mary Ann had bravely smiled through it all.

This pic... a nothing of a moment, the proverbial split second. A lie. The perfect, middle-class, All-American fam, perched on the dresser as a huge middle finger to the years of misery. Mary Ann's desperate claim to at least a C-minus in Mothering.

Or... was it possible that maybe this picture had captured the truth, and it was Vern himself who resisted it, who created the domestic chaos out of some need for power or meaning, out of fear of being loved or feeling worthy without external accolades? Maybe it was Vern who deserved the non-passing grades in Son-ship and Brothering.

He felt dizzy. He put the picture back with exacting

tenderness, right next to the stack of assisted living brochures he had foisted upon her at his last visit. He picked up the top one and knew that the pic on its cover, *this* pic, was the lie. Marketing copy. And for the first time in his life, he thought of his mother's future in the concrete rather than merely the abstract.

Holy shit. Mom was a *person*.

"Vern?" Bryce asked. "You ok?"

Vern couldn't speak. He looked at his little brother, and again the boundaries of space-time seemed to blur, and he saw a version of Bryce unsquelched by Vern's casual, self-serving, big-bro cruelty. And that Bryce looked like a pretty dapper fella. Not that people aren't ultimately responsible for their happiness, but the playing field for Bryce had never been level. Vern's thumb had tilted the scales from the moment Bryce was born.

His phone buzzed. He took it out.

"Driver, I'm with my family, I told you—"

Driver spoke quick. "Cliff Flagler just called and said get to the airport right away and the Gulfstream is ready and Sandy and Malcolm Sneed have invited you to dinner at their new country club in Orlando so get a move on."

Vern blinked. His threat had worked. If a deal could be hammered out tonight, maybe the fine citizens of Sawnichikee wouldn't have to miss their *Wheel of Fortune* tomorrow after all.

"Two minutes."

Vern hung up and looked to his mother, discovered her already glaring at him, perfectly lucid and spiteful. The small family existed in silence for a few moments before Mary Ann began to speak, pointing a crooked finger in Vern's direction.

"O ill-dispersing wind of misery! O my accursed womb, the

bed of death! A cockatrice hast thou hatch'd to the world, whose unavoided eye is murderous."

Vern was never good with metaphors and certainly was not fluent in Elizabethan, but his mother's intent was painfully clear.

"Oh, that deceit should steal such gentle shapes. He is my son; yea, and therein my shame; Yet from my dugs he drew not this deceit."

Silence, except for Mary Ann panting lightly. Vern, deep down, examined the reprimand, found it deserving, and accepted it.

"I'll visit again this weekend," he whispered. "We'll go to Yoder's for some pie."

"Why not now, Vern?" Bryce said.

Vern reached over to pat Bryce on the shoulder. With, y'know, *kindness*. But Bryce flinched, as he had been conditioned to do. Vern paused mid-pat. Again examined and accepted the reprimand. Almost said, "I'm sorry, my brother." But didn't.

"Next time, Bryce. There's something I have to do first."

See? He still thought he had time.

Don't we all?

18

THE AIRPORT

En route to the airport, Vern was feeling giddy and enlightened. Why had it taken him so long to realize he was in control? He was going to put the Sneeds in their place, get his campaign back on track, and fix his relationships with Mia, Mama, and Bryce, whip bam boom.

He chugged a Red Bull and put in a call to his ruefully put-upon aide. The poor kid had gone through unmitigated hell as a Chi Phi pledge but nothing could prepare him for the torture and humiliation he would endure in his first real-world employment as Vern Bushnell's whipping boy. On a normal day, Vern derived a great deal of glee from castigating his peons. Today? Feeling his oats? He hoped the phone wouldn't be answered promptly enough, giving him an excuse to throw his new sense of agency around, but unfortunately the young gudgeon picked up in two rings.

"Vern Bushnell's office. This is Scott Orth. How may I direct your call?"

"Scott!"

Scott gulped. "Sir?"

Vern glanced out the Escalade window as they passed the main terminal entrance. Season traffic was backed up to the main drag. Vern thanked his lucky stars he wasn't flying commercial. No doubt, clumsy dismounts and long goodbyes in the unloading zone were screwing countless vacations for people who hadn't planned for delays. Amateurs.

"Scotty!"

"Yes sir?"

"Scotty-Scott-Scott!

"Can you hear me, sir?"

"Loud and clear. I'm on my way to the airport."

"Great. Good to go, sir. The charter's all lined up. Bob Rowe's got her gassed up and—"

"You got somebody set to pick me up when I land?"

"Yes, sir. Lauren's already at MCO."

"Right on. Listen, Scotty. I'm not sure if I'll be staying the night in Orlando or coming back. Just in case I wrap this up quick and DO come back, it'll still be awful late, and I don't want to disturb the old lady. Can you call the Ritz and reserve my usual room?"

"Yes, sir. Sure thing. For tonight?"

"Scotty, yer killing me. How much did you pay for that fancy degree of yours? You got screwed, my man. What did I JUST say?"

At Bushnell HQ Scott Orth bit down on his hand to suppress a scream. "Yes, sir, I got it. And, sir? Cliff Flagler keeps calling the office. He really wants to talk to you. Says it's important."

Vern chuckled to himself. Ol' "Uncle Cliff" was scared shitless, too. This all was boding well.

"Okaaaay. Scotty, if he calls again, you just tell him I'll bring him back some Mickey Mouse ears."

"Yes, sir."

Without granting his aide the courtesy of a goodbye, Vern ended the call. Driver pulled the Escalade into Queen Palm Aviation and parked outside of the hangar. Vern got out and stretched. Driver handed over his luggage.

"Good luck, Congressman."

Vern grinned. His newly minted confidence must be radiating. Driver rarely employed such an honorific. "Thanks, Driver. I'll let you know if I need you to pick me up tonight."

Vern strode into the FBO as he had done hundreds of times before. Generally, Bob Rowe would be there chomping on an unlit Cuban cigar and would escort Vern to the Cessna, but today the lounge was empty. Maybe the Gulfstream took longer to prep.

"Hello?" Vern poked his head into the office. Empty. "Bob?"

No answer.

Vern walked back to the hangar, saw his Escalade about to pull away.

"Driver! You seen Bob?"

And then the most inexplicable thing happened. Driver leaned out the window, exposed his teeth in a violent grin, crossed his arms in the classic "screw you" gesture, and hollered back: "The name's *Harrison*, douchebag!" Then he stomped the gas and aimed for the nearest ATM to withdraw the big fat bonus Flagler had promised him. His part in the subterfuge was played, and a week or two in the Bahamas would be a great way to celebrate.

Vern's ego refused to acknowledge the shrieked warnings of his id. Surely there was a logical and Vern-empowering explanation. He took a step in the direction of the tarmac—perhaps Bob was waiting there, with the Gulfstream, that would fly him to Orlando, so he could take down the Sneeds a peg or two—but before he could take a second step, there appeared before him, seemingly from nowhere, a walking anachronism.

A man of indeterminate age. Hair buzzed in a savage crew cut. White short-sleeved dress shirt and clip-on tie. Archaic credentials hanging loosely from a pocket protector jammed with pens, pencils, and was that a protractor-compass combo? Vern rubbed his eyes. But the man was still there, looking like a misplaced NASA technician from the early 1960s.

"Good Afternoon, Congressman," the man said, with a tone that toed the line between genial and sinister.

The hairs on Vern's arms screeched upright. His gibbering id kicked his ego's shins hard enough for fight or flight to take effect. You all know Vern well enough at this point to know he chose flight, yes?

But as he dropped his luggage and made a graceless and panicky about-face, Vern was met with another man, a bit pudgy around the middle but otherwise identical to the first. Vern's stomach suddenly realized it had ingested an alarming variety of liquids over the previous few hours... Dickel, Arnold Palmer, OJ, Red Bull. Nausea overwhelmed his pride and he puked all over his shoes.

As he listened to the splatter, his ego finally concluded that two plus two is indeed four. So many times he'd heard stories of poor wretches who had run afoul of the powers that be, of the humiliating demises met by ridiculous men who'd fancied themselves Teflon. Now, the tale of Vern Bushnell would be added to the cautionary pile. He honestly thought he could outwit Uncle Cliff and take down the Sneeds? He'd been bested by his goddamn driver, for fuck's sake. The shock of this revelation rendered even meek resistance impossible.

"Take it easy, brother," said the first man as he patted Vern on the back. The pudgy man approached as well, pulling something from his pocket. And in incredibly short order Vern felt the sharp stab of a syringe in his neck. He could tell when each layer of his skin was being penetrated by the needle. Vern felt as though his head was going to explode as the potent serum traversed his venous return, entered his heart, got sent out to his lungs, returned from his lungs, exited his heart, climbed his carotids, and finally reached his brain. For about forty-five seconds Vern sputtered objections that made perfect sense to him but actually were unfettered gibberish. And then Vern Bushnell blacked out.

The strangely identical men dragged him to the tarmac and loaded him into a waiting Piper.

19

BIMINI CRICKET

A tropical storm was headed toward Port Royal and a few of the local rum enthusiasts had decided to hunker down at Enid's and wait out the storm there.

Enid's, structurally speaking, was only slightly more complex than a thatched hut. You couldn't technically say it was a thatched hut, but you certainly couldn't consider it much more durable. Nonetheless, there it stood as it had for over fifty years, oblivious to the barometer.

Ten minutes after the rain began to pelt the island, a Piper made an unsteady landing at the nearby airstrip and two men in short-sleeved shirts and clip-on ties, both conscious, carried a man in a teal windbreaker and discolored shoes, unconscious, into a waiting vehicle. A short while later the vehicle arrived at Enid's.

The rum enthusiasts at Enid's rarely saw anyone who wasn't local. It was especially rare to see three non-locals. And the spectacle of two non-locals dragging an unconscious non-local in a teal windbreaker was especially unusual. The Sneeds' hush fund would be picking up the rum tabs tonight.

The sentient non-locals dragged the torpid non-local toward the back of the tiny building where a ratty curtain masked a set of stairs that they descended. The existence of a subfloor in Bimini, notoriously below sea level, was as rare as a non-local in a teal windbreaker. And yet, here at Enid's, there were stairs leading down into the depths of the earth.

The trio was met at the foot of the stairs by a Dominican nurse with a stretcher. This nurse was so tall he had to hunch over a bit to avoid bopping his head on the ceiling. They laid old Vern out and rolled him down a hallway. Several yards down, the brick walls became sleek stainless steel and the lighting went from rustic third-world to mid-century institutional. The fluorescents made Vern's masterfully sprayed tan appear pallid.

A bit further down, the doors of a glimmering steel service elevator parted. The men rolled Vern into the chamber and the Dominican reached down from on high to scan a plastic card into an outmoded reader. Upon being met with a red blinking light, the Dominican swore and angrily re-swiped his card three, four, seven, twelve, seventeen times before he was granted a green light and was able to control the trajectory of the elevator. The descent was interminable.

The doors parted and they moved into a sterile anteroom of resplendent linoleum. The Dominican swiped his card into another reader and was, predictably, met with a blinking red light. Countless more attempts were met with no success. The Dominican muttered and hammered the door once with a frustrated fist.

The wall slid open.

Inside, the men found a lab of sorts. The analog ambiance suggested a slightly higher-budget Roger Corman film. All sorts of random tubes and lights and knobs and levers. Sad little black and white monitors projected a fuzzy picture of the linoleum anteroom. And to add even more authenticity to this glorious Cold War tableau were two wry octogenarians in, predictably, white short-sleeved shirts and black clip-on ties.

Vern's pudgier captor addressed the old men.

"Which of you is Agent Larchmont?"

"I'm Agent Emerson," said one of the old men, the one with the ambitious and pathetic comb-over. Some day he would acknowledge that he was balding, but today was not that day. "He's Larchmont." Emerson pointed at Larchmont.

Larchmont cleared his throat. He had a head of thick, tufted, salt-and-pepper hair. He pointed at himself. "Larchmont."

"Well, here he is."

The two old men approached Vern and began to prod him with their fingers.

"Our facsimile machine is giving us problems," Emerson said. "You'll have to fill us in a bit."

20

SHAKE YOUR BOOTY

The two abductors gave Emerson and Larchmont the skinny as the nurse strapped Vern, still unconscious, to a bizarre machine. If you squinted just so it looked like a medieval torture device, but this massive marvel of gadgetry was of unmistakably stainless steel Cold War design. The spaces in the machine designed to hold the appendages forced Vern's body into an upright, splayed-out X.

"So this comes down direct from the Sneeds, eh?" Emerson said as he fiddled with a wire attached to a suction cup attached to Vern's pelvis.

The first short-sleeved man glanced at his slightly pudgy twin and grunted. "Yeah. That's all we know. Just don't kill him and definitely don't lose him."

"Blah blah blah," Larchmont said. He flapped a hand at them. "We've got it."

The nurse escorted the two kidnappers out. Their job was done. Agents Emerson and Larchmont got down to business.

Emerson twisted dials and tracked Vern's vitals as Larchmont sat next to an old phonograph record player that was connected to Vern via a bevy of RCA cables and electrodes. He shuffled through the vinyl, trying this one and that one. Music echoed through the lab. The nurse bopped his head in time to the various beats. But nothing took.

An hour passed. Another. Larchmont riffled through a third crate of old records. A pile of discards lay at his feet. Emerson and the nurse methodically checked the electrodes peppering Vern's body.

"You sure he's plugged in right?" Larchmont said, running his hand yet again through his lush and increasingly frazzled hair.

"All great men must fall," Emerson hypothesized, "whether through their own folly or the actions of others."

"How about saying something useful, Emerson!" snapped Larchmont.

"I'm only saying—"

"Maybe concentrate on your work?"

"Good Christ, Dave. I'm trying to keep it light, just making conversation."

"But it's plebeian philosophy you're spouting and it gives me a headache."

They continued their work in silence. Then Emerson yanked off his clip-on tie and hurled it across the room.

"All of the connections are in place," Emerson said. The nurse nodded in agreement. "I don't get it!"

The men pondered things. Larchmont looked through the pile of discards.

"I've tried Diz and Dolphy. Bud Powell. Monk."

"The Four Freshmen?"

"Yes the Four fucking Freshmen. Brubeck."

"Max Roach?"

"Ah-ha!" Larchmont looked up with gleaming eyes. "I haven't tried Max Roach."

Larchmont stepped over the first crate, stubbed his toe on the second, grabbed the fourth, stacked it on top of the third. He plunged his hands into the dustjackets and pulled out an album. Emerson flipped a switch on the Cold War contraption and it glowed blue. Larchmont started the record. It played a very loud Max Roach solo. The men and the nurse looked hopefully at the ancient EKG.

Flatlines. The primal rhythms affected Vern not at all. The music reached a crescendo. Still nothing.

From behind a dividing screen came a new, gruff, hyper-masculine voice.

"Can you boys light a fire under it, for Chrissake?"

"Put a lid on it, pops!" Larchmont shouted at the voice behind the screen, and then he mumbled "Maybe we oughta try some Mingus..."

The screen whipped open and another octogenarian emerged. He, like Vern, was connected to dated equipment through intimately placed electrodes. He brusquely yanked himself free, ignoring Emerson's plea to "take it easy on those!" He stalked over to Vern's X-ed body, wires dangling from his virile body like tentacles.

"Can we do this thing sometime before next year?"

"Can it, D'Angelo!" Larchmont said.

D'Angelo growled. Larchmont blanched.

"Can we all just calm down?" Emerson said. "We'll figure out his trigger, we just have to be patient."

The nurse sat on a stool in the corner, stretched out his impossibly long legs, and unwrapped a candy bar.

D'Angelo's glare carried weight. His uncommonly high cheekbones had become more pronounced through the years and his hair was full-on white, but aside from these indicators of agedness the march of time barely registered on him. He moved fluidly, whereas Emerson and Larchmont, several years his junior, creaked with every step. Somehow his muscles still retained definition, nothing dangled or wobbled. Physically he was a damn *specimen*. After such a long and redacted career with various shadowy agencies, you'd think he would have mastered the art of patience. But no. His youthful antsiness maintained well into obsolescence.

"What's the fuggin' hold up, gentlemen?"

Emerson whined. "This kid's pineal glands are like granite!"

D'Angelo began to poke around Vern's setup.

"D'Angelo!" howled Larchmont. "Step away!"

D'Angelo ignored him. Poked. Prodded. Turned Vern's head to the side and took a good pensive look at his profile.

"He looks like my nephew."

"He's not your nephew, D'Angelo." Larchmont drew himself up. "Now get back to your cot and plug yourself back in!"

D'Angelo elbowed Larchmont out of the way and flipped through the albums.

Larchmont wheezed as Emerson clucked like a mother hen.

"D'Angelo, man... Didn't we talk about this? Boundaries? Remember?"

"Well somebody's gotta get this thing going. Here." D'Angelo handed Emerson an album. "I've known punks like this."

Then, self-assurance oozing (and if the two scientists were honest with themselves they'd admit they were fiendishly jealous of said ooze), D'Angelo trotted back to his cot and reconnected his electrodes to the archaic mainframe.

Emerson and Larchmont looked at the album. Larchmont read the cover with difficulty, as if it were written in another language:

"Kaaay Seeee? And the Sunshine Band?"

Emerson pinched the bridge of his nose and shook his head. "No no no no WAY, D'Angelo."

"Trust me, dipshits. Spin it up."

A softly accented voice floated in from the corner, words gooey with partially chewed nougat. "Play that funky music, white boys," said the Dominican nurse.

D'Angelo cackled. Emerson heaved a sigh. Larchmont looked around as though lost.

"Might as well give it a try, Dave," Emerson said.

With considerable resignation, Larchmont put the album on the turntable and dropped the needle.

Do a little dance! Make a little love!

The effects were immediately apparent. The EKG spiked. The heart monitor revved. Vern's strapped-down limbs strained, held back in their attempts to boogie and screw.

"Crank the volume, boys!" D'Angelo hollered.

Get down tonight! Get down tonight!

Vern's eyes fluttered. D'Angelo knew—having taken many of these journeys before—that at this moment Vern was as close to transcendence as a human could get, glorying in the hyper-reality of his most blissful memory, which probably meant Vern was once again young and unabashedly randy and unencumbered by legislative pitfalls, driving his black and orange Z-28 at reckless speeds while shirtless and eight Miller High Lifes under.

Do a little dance! Make a little love!

"Well whaddya know," Larchmont muttered.

Emerson had his nose buried in flashing monitors. "His pineal glands are decalcified! Limbic pulsations accelerating! Prepare for transfer!"

Get down tonight! Get down tonight!

Now that they had Vern locked and loaded, as it were, the giddy scientists had but one more undertaking remaining before they could pull the trigger. They would track the vectors of Vern's limbic pulsations—whatever the fuck *those* are—to identify a suitable destination. That is, a parallel universe in which there was neither hide nor hair of any version of Vern Bushnell.

21

THE ORIGINS OF "THE PROJECT"

I f you're anything like me, you want to know a bit more about this ornery duo, the Agents Larchmont and Emerson, and exactly what forces of the natural world they were futzing with. The technobabble is infuriating and I think intentionally opaque. So here's a nutshell for you.

The most ironic thing about The Project is that the very man who covertly instituted the endeavor was also the unwitting first subject. John Fitzgerald Kennedy had done a bit of reading. And his friend, screen legend Cary Grant, had mentioned the "Larchmont and Emerson Experiments" as they lazed by a pool in Palm Springs.

And John Kennedy, whom we can all at least agree was pragmatic, considered the notion itself and how it could be employed in matters of the state. What use could the existence of alternate and parallel universes provide? He didn't care about the technical differences between "alternate" and "parallel," by the way. Chaos or string theory? Pshaw. Multiverse? Yawn. He saw the bigger picture. Wide-open spaces, far from the prying eyes of newly launched satellites and fickle voters?

What could be accomplished with such brimming social laboratories? Make the moon landing look like an Easy-Bake Oven.

Even as a Catholic it never occurred to him to consider the Project's implications to our understanding of the "soul." Did every "JFK" across all these universes become President and sneak in quickies with Marilyn? Nope. But "they" were not really "he," right? Heck, think about what he coulda figured out if he'd sought out the Moseses and Jesuses and Muhammads.

But he didn't. He was more interested in holding cells. The Kennedys had plenty of lukewarm acquaintances who were loose enough cannons to be wary of. The Kennedys were also in possession of enough savvy to know that some of these people were inherently useful to them, whether through their unique skills or specialized knowledge, and were indispensable despite being obvious liabilities.

In a singular universe, this was problematic because they had to weigh value and utility against the possibility that a peripheral cog might up and tell the whole world about some sordid weekend in Monaco or Chappaquiddick. But the existence of accessible multiple universes meant a person could be "'gotten rid of" but kept alive and accessible in a veritable bilge tank. Like storing blackmail in a safety deposit box in the trippiest bank ever.

There were kinks to be worked out. First, a method by which to locate a universe wherein the dispatched did not already exist. For whatever metaphysical reasons, you didn't want to double-dip. Early experiments when the quantum void was not respected resulted in some spectacularly messy outcomes. Ever seen someone turn inside out in real-time? Egads.

And, of course, a bigger kink: the question of how to maintain contact with the subject once appropriately dispatched and make sure you don't misplace them. Even today, GPS trackers go haywire outside the universe in which they were manufactured. The tech hasn't caught up, so same as Day One it's analog all the way. But if you have to send a "babysitter" along with every subject—someone to maintain surveillance— what if said babysitter already exists in the universe where the subject does not? This led to a lot of agents trading voids. "I'll kill your *you* in THAT universe if you kill my *me* in THIS one." The spreadsheets were epic.

But eventually, things got sufficiently systemized, and Larchmont and Emerson were given a small contingent of newly-minted federal agents who had been carefully vetted for patriotism and lack of philosophical scruples. These eager youngsters were given haircuts and crisp white shirts and clip-on ties and were trained in the clandestine procedures that would disappear a bevy of indispensable enemies to democracy over the years.

Including—and this is the ironic part—in 1963, JFK himself, who had come to hold less sway over The Project than certain other people who felt that he was turning out to be something of a loose cannon himself.

22

LARCHMONT'S EARLY DAYS

Stan Larchmont had moved to the westernmost reaches of Greenwich Village from Evansville, Indiana, in the mid-1950s because he wanted to be a poet. At that time the Village was composed almost entirely of poets, so it seemed like a reasonable place for a poet to go to drown in obscurity. Had poetry continued to demand Larchmont's vocational attention, he would've drowned in obscurity with aplomb. Fortunately, his poet's acumen for grasping abstract concepts served him well in what would be his life's work.

It all began when he saw Bud Powell play at a little joint on MacDougal Street. Bud was in a syncopated trance behind an upright piano when a man in a banquette near the stage began to quiver and froth. The bartender and one of the waiters, as if they'd done it a hundred times, swooped in and gently whisked him out of the club. Bud Powell didn't flinch.

When the waiter came back to the table with the next round of drinks, Larchmont asked him if the guy was alright. "Sure," said the waiter. "Just had his mind blown is all."

Larchmont heard in the waiter's voice a statement of fact.

The man's mind had been blown by Bud Powell. This was no mere turn of phrase. It was literal. And it happened to people all the time when Bud played. This got Larchmont to thinking some very profound thoughts as he sipped his drink. Some of them were:

"Music is the purest expression of mathematics."

"Music is a conduit for the soul."

"The soul is elusive."

"The Far East and even the North American Continent were once elusive but through advances in astronomy, magnetism, and physics... they were found."

These thoughts coalesced into an intoxicating "what if." Perhaps, Larchmont posited, the soul could also be found. Perhaps music, being both of pure, hard numbers and soft, transcendent intangibles, was bestowed upon humankind as a sort of compass.

He thought he had the makings of a great poem in there somewhere. In actuality, he had taken his first steps toward his new scientific calling. Observe. Hypothesize.

Larchmont returned to the little joint on MacDougal night after night, waiting for another mind to be blown so that he might be able to ascertain where the soul was and what it was trying to communicate. Larchmont smoked a lot of tea in those days.

Well, one night there was a surprise visit from Max Roach and, on that night, minds were blown en masse. It began with an especially primal snare solo during "Softly as in a Morning Sunrise," when a woman standing to the right of the stage was overtaken. Her face began to contort, her eyes grew bright as spotlights, and then her pupils disappeared into the back of her head. She swayed back and forth for a bit, then gracefully collapsed to the floor. Not a second later a man sitting at a deuce in front of the stage began to vibrate and writhe. His ladyfriend reached for him but before she could make contact her mind was blown, too. She ground her thighs together audibly and began to coo. The same happened at the table next to them. Larchmont watched it spread from there. He and the bartender were the only two souls in the place somehow unaffected. It was nearly forty-five minutes later when everyone came to.

When the coat check girl came around, her eyelids fluttering, her cheeks glowing, her eyes sparkling with enlightenment, Larchmont rushed to her.

"What happened?" he said.

She exhaled. Her breath smelled of the cosmos. "I went..." She swooned.

Larchmont caught her. He shook her lightly and asked, "Went? Where? *Where??*"

Her gaze went inside him and through him. "I was everywhere, Pops. Simply everywhere."

23

A BIT ABOUT EMERSON

Emerson was not a modest man when he was young. Once a month he took his father's car from Bensonhurst to Murray Hill, New Jersey, and demanded to speak to Mervin Kelly, the President of Bell Labs. He had some ideas about how to "revolutionize our understanding of vacuum tubes." A bold thing to say to Mervin Kelly. And ineffective at first. But finally, after the most obnoxious level of persistence, Kelly agreed to meet with Emerson, if only to shut him up.

Now, Emerson's ideas were truly outlandish. Science fiction pulp. Kelly let Emerson deliver his vacuum diatribe for five minutes and had him sized up. The kid was bright and confident and had a degree from Columbia. The kid was also a real nudge. He would drive everyone crazy. But Kelly was wise enough to know that nudges are usually good for at least one bright idea every three years or so. If nothing else, relentless blue-sky ramblers keep the working stiffs honest.

So Kelly took Emerson in at Bell Labs, and Emerson was sure he was going to change the world. But within days

William goddamn Gardner Pfann announced "Zone Melting" and it was all anyone talked about. Emerson's ideas languished, not just warily side-eyed but completely ignored. He even found himself at one point stuffing envelopes. By his fourth year at The Bell, the obsequious knobs in the Transistor Department took home the Nobel Prize and, again, Emerson's light was under a bushel. *Transistors?* Did they not even see what was right under their noses? And under their feet? And surrounding them? These pockets of weightless matter that people call air? But all they could talk about was making things smaller. *Things.*

At a particularly low point, Emerson was wandering the streets of Greenwich after getting into a fistfight with one of the groomsmen at a wedding for some distant cousin. He fell into a coffee shop on Waverly. Larchmont was also there, wrestling with his poem that wasn't a poem. A smoke was bummed. A light was given. A conversation was born.

On such small, seemingly random moments do great events turn.

The two men actually didn't like each other, and never would. But they saw and heard in each other a mutual way forward. Sum and parts. Larchmont regaled Emerson with his ungodly patter about how he'd once seen the future whilst listening to a boss arrangement of "Night in Tunisia." Emerson wanted details and grew frustrated when Larchmont was unable to put it into even vaguely scientific terms, but it all fed into his trip on how *things* needn't exist. He ranted about vacuums. Larchmont composed on the spot a sonnet about nothingness. Emerson rolled his eyes and ordered another Americano. The two men talked and argued and belittled and provoked each other for several hours.

When they came out the other end, the sun was beginning

to rise over distant Hoboken, and the men had formed a part-
nership that would endure, albeit with no small amount of
mutual hostility, five decades and counting.

24

FINDING A UNIVERSE WITHOUT VERN

A rtie Bushnell met Mary Anne Spitzmueller in 1957. On the evening of May 28th, 1963 Artie—in a rare show of ardor—made his wife pregnant. Early the next year Vern was born.

No good. Not helpful.

Artie Bushnell met Mary Anne Spitzmueller in 1957. On the evening of May 28th, 1963, Mr. and Mrs. Bushnell had gone to dinner at the Westerner Beef Buffet on Michigan Avenue and Artie had sprung for a bottle of wine and laid the charm on real thick. Before she knew it, Mary Anne was pregnant with her son, Vern.

Nope. No dice.

Artie Bushnell met Mary Anne Spitzmueller in the summer of 1957. She had just finished watching her sister sing 'Ave Maria' at St. Sebastian's and was walking down Merrick Street when he pulled up next to her in his father's Nash Rambler and told her to get in. They were married the next year. On the evening of May 28th, 1963, after the Lloyd Bridges Show, Artie and Mary Anne got into the schnapps and, in due time, they had a baby boy named Vern.

Useless.

When Artie saw Mary Anne for the first time, his internal reaction was unlike anything he had ever experienced. It was unmistakable. Though he was not an impulsive man, he knew beyond a doubt that this would be the woman who would share his bed until he died. This would be the woman that would give up dancing for him, and humor him when he drank too much, and darn his socks, and heat up his Salisbury steak, and listen to him drone on about catalytic converters, and give him two sons. One, Vern. The other, Bryce. Vern, their first, was conceived on May 28th, 1963, and after a solid eight and a half months of gestation, entered the world.

Dammit.

The Quantum-Twin Implosion Preventer sped through scenario after scenario like that. Thousands, hundreds of thousands, over a million realities, constantly varied in ways overt or tiny, but each with the same blasted outcome: Vern Bushnell was born.

Reality one million, seven hundred and forty-three sped by on the split flash display. A blob of green code. Gibberish to you or me, but to the frazzled scientists, each batch of rowed and columned numbers and letters was a snapshot of another universe. And somehow another Vern.

Flash. Vern.

Flash. Vern.

Flash. Vern.

Emerson and Larchmont began to think something had come loose in their trusty, ancient machine. Never before had they encountered a soul as tenacious as this one. "Mathematical oddity" didn't even come close. For a blessed union as lackluster and devoid of romance as Artie and Mary Anne's, it endured all quantum variables. And Vern's incarnation, as aimless and ignoble as it seemed, was more certain in every scenario than Chernobyl, the election of Jimmy Carter, the Jackson Five Victory Tour, and the Atkin's diet. Until finally, after nineteen and a half hours—D'Angelo had even gone out for a constitutional and a steak, you typically didn't want to transfer on anything but an empty stomach, but this was getting ridiculous—the split flash display spit up scenario one million, five hundred thirty-three thousand, two hundred and seventeen:

On May 28th, 1963, Artie and Mary Anne Bushnell of Dear-
born Heights, Michigan, were playing backgammon at the
kitchen table. They'd been drinking quite a bit. He was drinking
gin and she was having too much kirschwasser than she should.
Artie interspersed his cocktails with glass bottles of Coca-Cola.
By eleven-thirty they were ginned up, kirschwassered up, and
Artie was wired on Coca-Cola to boot. Artie took Mary Anne
right there in the kitchen, but during a key moment of the coitus
the lactic acid from all of that Coca Cola, and the awkward
angle of his approach, conspired to give Artie the most painful
charley horse he had ever experienced. He lay on the kitchen
floor, pants around his ankles, howling in pain.

"Jesus!" he cried.

"What can I do? What can I do to help?" Mary Anne
thought he was having a heart attack but, between grunts, he told
her this used to happen in college and he just needed to walk it
off. She helped him up and he hobbled around, trying to stretch
his leg and pull up his pants at the same time.

"I'm sorry, baby," said Artie.

"It's alright," said Mary Anne, "Some other time."

She held him up while he limped back and forth. After his
cramp abated, they went to bed. And then to sleep.

BINGO! A Vern-less universe!

A light went on and a little bell went off, wresting Larchmont and Emerson from their argument.

"Is that? Is that?!" Emerson said.

Larchmont whacked him a good one on the back. "Eureka!"

"About damned time!" D'Angelo said. The nurse helped
him hastily reapply his electrodes.

Emerson promptly set the coordinates as Larchmont

released the lock, tilted Vern back to a 45-degree angle, and undid all the straps. They and the nurse all put on protective goggles. Then together they carefully opened the panel in the floor, just beneath Vern's feet. There, a wormhole swirled, not quite liquid, not quite vacuum, not quite anything. I've tried many times to describe it, but no can do. Just think of the most acid-laced image you can, whether the last part of *2001 Space Odyssey*, or the parading elephants in *Fantasia*, or your local planetarium's cheesy attempt to underscore its laser light show with Pink Floyd. Then add a ton of nausea, the best orgasm of your life, and the very real sense of drowning, and you might come close.

I'll put it another way. The goggles weren't to stop gamma rays or anything like that. They had become standard protocol after the first nurse, way back in 1961, had looked into the wormhole sans goggles and promptly gone insane.

Larchmont, Emerson, and the nurse folded Vern's arms across his chest, detached all the wires, and guided his fleshy valise of neurons and hubris straight into the depths of infinity. Like depositing a check with the bank teller's pneumatic tube.

The transfer yanked Vern into consciousness, but he had no context for this experience. He screamed but heard no sound, not even in his head. He hurled through an abstract landscape at great speed, flailing, falling. Or, since observation is based on the subjective idea of "stationary," Vern flailed in place at zero velocity as the abstract landscape whizzed past him. On the seeming cyclorama of the horizon images from his life moved in counter-chronological order, accelerating and telescoping and zeroing in.

Adulthood. Teen angst. Childhood.

Vern saw a hospital room.

A tub of water.

A gaping vagina.

Light disappeared as he entered. He sensed but could not see the warm womb.

Then his consciousness compressed, and way off in the pitch dark the merest flicker of meager light *pfff'd* into existence. It grew and grew. The vice on his awareness squeezed and squeezed. The light began to pierce. The pressure and the light became one. The light was so bright and the pressure so tight... they began to emit sound. And that's when Vern realized he was afraid. The sound pounded. The light blinded. Vern was so squeezed he felt his very self disappearing. All he knew was vibration, the heartbeat of the cosmos, and he suddenly experienced first-hand how energy could be both wave and particle at the same time. His very matter defied being.

And then, just like that, quite literally, *nothing*.

25

VERN WAKES UP

Vern snapped awake from a mind-blowing fever dream of sacred geometry and time goo. His eyes fluttered for several moments as his surroundings came into focus. He was sitting on vinyl. Sun refracted through a window onto his face. There was the distant sound of large engines. An airport? A vaguely familiar airport? Queen Palm airport! The main terminal. What possible reason would he have to be in the main terminal with the hoi polloi? He stood up. He wobbled dangerously, regained his balance, and reached for his luggage. None to be had. Where the hell was his luggage? And Driver? Had Driver just left him here in the goddamn main terminal without his luggage??

And was Driver's name... *Harrison*?? How did he know that?

Vern took a deep calming breath. He slapped his cheeks and shook his head to clear the wooziness. It didn't work. His stomach felt like it was trying to climb up this throat. He looked around more carefully, then made his way toward an information kiosk where a silver-haired volunteer was tidying a display of brochures.

"Good morning, sir," she said. Her voice was like the chirp of a small bird. It drilled a hole in Vern's head. "How may I be of assistance?"

"Hi there, yeah, I think I've gotten a little turned around here. Can you tell me how to get back to Queen Palm Aviation?"

"I'd be happy to assist you, sir." Her fingers hovered at the ready over a keyboard. "Do you have an address for—?"

"It's here. At the airport."

"Oh, forgive me. Could you repeat the name of the, uh..."

"Queen. Palm. Aviation."

"Queen Palm?"

God her *voice*. Chirp chirp chirp, stab stab stab. He pressed a knuckle into his eye and took another calming breath.

"Yes, yes, Queen Palm. Queen Palm Aviation. The FBO. The lounge. The private, uh... I have a charter flight."

"Oh, a charter! Well let me just run that through the Google. One moment, please."

Her nails pecked at the keys. Peck peck peck.

"Can you just—? It's *here*. Right here at this airport. What the hell kind of information desk is this?"

The computer dinged. The woman chirped. "Do you mean Dolphin Aviation?"

"What? No, I don't mean Dolphin damn Aviation. Queen Palm Aviation!"

She smiled a tight smile and pecked again—it took ages—and then shook her head. "I'm very sorry, sir. I'm not coming up with any 'Queen Palm Aviation.' Would you like me to—"

"No, god, no, thank you, never mind. I'll find it myself."

He stalked away, but not without one last stab to the back of his head. "Enjoy your flight!"

Vern patted his pockets and discovered that he'd misplaced his iPhone. Probably left it in the Escalade. He muttered a series of compound profanities and willed the nausea to ease up. Moving deliberately through the airport, he asked anyone who seemed to be there in any official capacity how to get to Queen Palm Aviation and was met with a stream of affable shrugs.

He approached the baggage claim. A sign caught his eye. He stopped dead in his tracks and his tummy once again tried to exit through his sinuses. The sign was so unnerving because it seemed to insist that he was not, as he had been assuming, at QPN (Queen Palm Regional Airport), but was instead at SKC (Sawnichikee Regional Airport).

Vern turned and sprinted for the nearest sliding glass doors. He emerged from the airport onto a sidewalk, leaned over with hands on knees, and gulped the familiar salt-soaked air.

"There there, Vern," he said to himself. "Just too much excitement and day-drinking. Get a grip now." He made a silent promise to cut back on the booze and get back to spin class. He straightened up and promptly was overcome with an even more profound sense of dislocation. He dropped to his backside on the concrete as his legs gave out. He looked around, flummoxed beyond reckoning.

He couldn't remember the last time he'd been anywhere near the main terminal, but things were utterly outta whack. Where there once had been a parking lot chock full of cars, there was now a vast green pasture with smatterings of topiary. Children played, families picnicked, a flag football game was underway. It occurred to Vern that perhaps he had gone out the wrong exit. But no. Any other exit would have emptied onto the runway. And he would have certainly known, given his close association with the Airport Board, if an enormous green space like this had been proposed and voted on much less established.

A concerned skycap made the mistake of checking on the man sitting smack in the middle of the sidewalk. Vern accosted him noisily.

"You! Tell me!"

"How can I help you, sir?"

"Where's Queen Palm Aviation?"

"I don't know, sir. Do you need some help? Here."

The skycap reached out his hand but Vern batted it away—"Nevermind!!"—and staggered to his feet. The very earth seemed to tilt beneath him.

"Sir, are you sure you don't—?"

But Vern had already trudged away, weaving like a drunk on a sloop in the chop. He made his way on foot around the perimeter of the airport and across a field of sand spurs. He avoided looking directly at anything because every time he did he felt his axis tilt. After about a quarter-mile marching north he reached the entrance to the private hangars. There he found a securely locked ramshackle warehouse that was entirely the wrong color, some run-down hangars housing a few decrepit old single engines, but no Gulfstream, and no Escalade in the parking lot.

"What the Sam fucking Hill is happening around here??"

He hiked back to the main terminal where the skycap kept a safe distance but still assisted him in securing a cab to the Ritz Carlton.

Vern sank gratefully into the back seat and blasting a/c. The cab pulled away from the airport.

"Here for business or pleasure, sir?" said the cabbie.

"Um. I don't know. I can't quite—"

Then the cab turned onto Tamiami Trail and Vern couldn't speak. Oh, he had a million thoughts, but verbalizing any of them was out of the question. He pressed his face to the window and watched the wholly unfamiliar landscape roll by. Well, not *wholly* unfamiliar. Tamiami Trail still ran northerly-southerly but it was eerily devoid of traffic. And the buildings, the blessed skyscrapers and dazzling condominiums that had risen so gracefully and expediently during Vern's run of things, were quite absent. Actually, non-existent would be more accurate, since "absent" would imply they had one time before been present in this universe, which they had not. Vern of course didn't understand this distinction. Not yet. Instead, as he peered up and down the street and into the passing neighborhoods, he saw the tattered but charming architecture that had existed, for him, pre-Queen Palm. Modest buildings of Spanish and Mediterranean inspiration. Somehow, dear, old Sawnichikee had been resurrected.

Vern finally found some words. But they left the cabbie baffled.

"How did the historical society pull this shit off?"

26

VERN IS TURNED AWAY AT THE RITZ-CARLTON

W hen the cab arrived at the Ritz-Carlton, Vern reached into his pocket and found that along with the sleek architectural trappings of modern Queen Palm and his iPhone, his wallet was also gone.

The cabbie was far more gentle and gracious than he had any right to be, having endured Vern's profanity-laced commute. He agreed to wait a few minutes while Vern checked in and "got oriented." As Vern turned to head inside, however, an early model Buick Regal pulled up behind the cab. A lean old man in a short-sleeved dress shirt, black clip-on tie, and dangling credentials stepped out. He gave off the coiled energy of a snake about to strike. He gave Vern the merest nod.

Vern's brain stem went haywire. The sunlight swirled around him and again his upchuck threat assessment red-lined. He backed away, gulping and shaking his head, and aimed his uncooperative feet at the Ritz entrance.

D'Angelo watched Vern go. He chuckled. He paid the cab driver and sent him on his way. Then he leaned against his

Buick, lit a cigarette, and waited for the fallout from the inevitable meltdown.

Vern somehow navigated his way through the door. He took healthy advantage of the complimentary beverage station just inside the entrance. A large crystal container of water with ice and many slices of cucumber bobbing inside sat next to a piping hot pot of coffee. He downed three glasses of the water in rapid succession, bringing on a blissful brain freeze that cut through the insistent deja vu. The tremble in his hands was barely noticeable as he poured coffee into a paper travel cup, slipped on the heat sleeve, and took a sip. It was good and strong, burning down his throat like elixir. He approached the front desk with a bit of his old swagger.

A curly-haired brunette looked up. "Hello, my name is Delia, welcome to the Ritz. How can I assist you today?"

Within a few seconds, Vern had judged that the new girl— he had never seen *Delia* before and he knew every concierge at this place—had been let off the leash too early.

"Ringling Suite, and quickly please, Delia."

"I'm afraid the Ringling suite is occupied," she said with a bright, corporate smile.

"It's supposed to be occupied, Delia. By me." His gut clenched again. Nausea ascended his windpipe. "My aide made a reservation."

"Yes, sir. It was Mr. Bushnell, correct?"

"Yep."

"Yes, very good, again, welcome to the Ritz. But as I said, we do not have a reservation in your name."

Vern gritted his teeth. Scott Orth had dropped the ball. That Clemson jackass. He'd done this on purpose, Vern would bet his life on it. Orth was a cocky little climber. And he carried body spray with him everywhere he went. It had been pure folly to take him on in the first place, but he was some donor's brother's nephew or somesuch. Vern sighed. Heavy weighs the crown.

Delia interrupted his fantasy of dressing down Scott in front of the whole office. "Mr. Bushnell, we do have lots of other rooms available."

"Fine. Just give me one on a high floor, facing the water."

"We'd be more than happy to accommodate you. Photo ID and credit card, please."

Vern leaned one arm onto the desk and unleashed his "I approved this message" grin. "Well, see that's the bitch of the situation, Delia. I seem to have lost my wallet. But let's just say I have a running tab at this hotel and we'll take care of the paperwork when my aide gets here."

Delia was impervious to his charms. "Oh, I'm afraid we don't have 'running tabs' here, sir."

But for Vern they did. Of *course* they did. He sipped more coffee, trying to keep calm.

"If you've stayed here before, though, Mr. Bushnell, perhaps I can find you in the system?"

"If I've stayed here before?? IF? Delia, you listen close now. I had a goddam fundraiser at this hotel not even two weeks ago! Dropped a half mil here, for Chrissake. In one night!"

His voice echoed across the highly polished lobby. The look on Delia's face, combined with the sudden sense of every eye in the place spotlighting onto him, kept Vern barely in check.

"I'm sorry, Delia. Truly. Look, would you let me use your phone?"

"Of course, Mr. Bushnell."

As Vern dialed, a family of tourists came in. Plainly Canadians. Delia—who it just so happened actually was new to this position, only her third week on the job—was instinctively prescient at that moment about how awkward this was about to get. These poor, unassuming Canucks, already reddened and peeling from poor SPF choices, were about to walk into a good jostling. Vern spoke stridently into the receiver.

"Who is this? Becky? This is Congressman Bushnell and I need to talk to Scott Orth right damn now. Orth. O-R-T-H. *Scott.* You don't know—? Are you from the staffing company? OK, Becky, I need you to stop talking and listen to me. I have lost my wallet. I need you to get the office AmEx and reserve a room for me here at the Queen Palm Ritz. Queen Palm. NO, not... ok, fine, sure the Sawnichikee Ritz."

Vern's composure shredded. He held on to his indignation for dear life.

"And make sure Scott Orth calls my room as soon as he gets to the office! Becky. Becky. BECKY! I am the *Congressman.* You're slicing off your bacon in my office, alright? I'm sorry to take this tone with you. I know you're new. But I am having a very trying day and I need you to just say 'Yes, sir. I'm on it.' Alright? Now I'm going to put you on with the young lady at the desk, here, her name is Delia, and I'd like you to reserve a room for me."

He handed over the receiver. "Unbelievable," he muttered.

Delia took the phone from him carefully, with two fingers, as if it was coated in phlegm.

"Hello?"

Vern tapped his fingers on the desk. Delia looked him up and down.

"Well, he says he's the Congressman. Vern Bushnell. No?" Delia covered the receiver with her hand. "Sir, I'm terribly sorry, but she says Park Robinson is the Congressman."

"Park Robinson?!" howled Vern. "That bottom feeder? Give me the damn phone!" He snatched the phone and snarled, "Becky, you're really beginning to piss me off—!" He looked at the phone in his hand, uncomprehending. "She hung up."

Delia desperately tried to recall all the de-escalation training from orientation a month back. "I'm very sorry, sir."

"You're *sorry?*"

Vern spotted a well-dressed middle-aged couple coming into the lobby. He called to them. "Excuse me!"

"Sir, please don't—"

"Excuse me!" He slammed down the phone and charged at the unassuming couple. Delia immediately picked the phone back up and dialed an extension.

"Who am I?" Vern asked the quaking couple. "Excuse me, Madame? Sir? You know who I am? Who am I??"

They looked at him like he was deranged and bolted into an elevator. Vern turned back to the desk.

"What's that you're doing? Who are you calling?"

He turned to the family of sunburned Canadians who had been waiting with sweet, northern-neighbor patience this entire time.

"Who am I? Tell her who I am!" he begged.

The mother put her arms around the children. The father bristled, which in Canadian meant he shrugged and smiled without teeth.

Delia hung up and did her best to intervene. "Sir, please, I really must insist you—"

Vern knelt and spoke patronizingly to the children.

"I am an elected official."

"Like a Prime Minister?" one of the children sing-songed.

"Sure, yes, kinda, see I go to Washington D.C. and make sure that our countries get along and that your mommy and daddy don't get screwed by European tariffs—"

Suddenly two Loss Prevention Officers emerged from out of nowhere in company-issued blazers and slacks. Vern was aghast. He turned to Delia with a wounded expression. "You called security? On *me?*"

"Sir, I'm going to have to ask you to leave the premises."

Camel's back, meet last straw.

"And I'm going to have to tell you to fuck right off! I'm not going anywhere! After almost a decade of loyal patronage—"

"Sir, you are trespassing on private property. I am at liberty to use physical force if necessary—"

"And that's just what you're going to have to do! I have never in all my days been treated with such—"

The Loss Prevention Officers, burly fellows both, each grabbed one of Vern's arms, lifted him off the ground, and headed to the front doors. A nearby bellman dutifully opened the door and the officers threw Vern out of the hotel. Vern stood up and screamed back at them, "You've just kissed your jobs goodbye! I play golf with your GM! He'll hear all about this! You can count on that!"

"You have a nice day, sir," said the bellman. Say this for the Ritz: their people stay cool.

Vern shook his fist. Then he stood in place. He had zero idea what to do next. Then he heard a slow clapping. He spun around and spotted D'Angelo, still leaning against the old Buick, regarding Vern's antics with amusement. Unaware of who D'Angelo was at this point, Vern puffed out his chest and bellowed, "What the hell are you looking at?"

D'Angelo didn't even flinch. He just grinned, flicked a lit Doral into some philodendron, and gave Vern an ironic salute.

27

VERN WALKS THE STREETS OF SAWNICHIKEE IN SPITE OF THE FACT THAT HE DOESN'T EXIST

Even if his wallet weren't missing, there's no way Vern could wait around the Ritz for a cab. Not after he'd been so humiliated. He stormed off the property and jay-walked across Tamiami Trail. He focused on his rage and kept his head down—everything still felt wonky when he looked too closely. So he didn't take much note of the glaring omissions from Queen Palm's skyline as he stomped up First Street and veered onto Pineapple Avenue. The changes in the urban topography only fully registered when Vern arrived at the corner where his condo was supposed to be.

He reached for the door, then froze. He backed up two steps and looked up and tried not to hyperventilate. He hadn't seen this view from this corner in years. Giant mounds of clouds so close you could reach out and grab 'em, lazing underneath that only-in-Florida, achingly blue sky. If he was able to see this much sky from this downtown corner, it meant his condo building was gone. And indeed it was. In its place stood Merlin's Bar, a Depression-Era holdout, defiantly mocking him.

Vern had personally witnessed Merlin's demolition, and yet here it stood. A brick and mortar ghost.

Vern stood blinking for several seconds. Then he went inside.

The bartender greeted him and put a bev-nap down on the bar. Vern took in his surroundings. They were *so* familiar, even if off by two degrees. He'd loved this place as a 20-something before he got rich and powerful tearing down places like this. Tearing down this place. The chicken wings alone, my god, the *wings.*

"What the fuck...?" he asked himself.

"Something to drink, sir?"

"I... I live here..."

"I'm also a native," said the bartender. "Heck of a town. Hope the secret doesn't get out. Traffic already gets snaggly enough when the snowbirds come down." He gave Vern a chuckle and a wink.

"I mean, I actually... You see it's..."

The bartender waited patiently for some sort of instruction and finally said, "Beer? Margarita?"

"Yes... that'll be fine."

"Well, which one? Or both? Ha! I don't judge, man."

Vern pressed his palms against his temples to keep his head from exploding.

"Nevermind... Thank you," said Vern. He weakly walked out of the bar.

Outside, Vern scanned the environs desperately. The sun was constant, there was that. As was the general geography. The handful of cars that passed him, while certainly not luxury models, reflected modernity. Tourists mingled with year-rounders, but the tourists looked more apt to go fishing and boating than golfing, and the year-rounders' fashion choices skewed far more toward chillaxed, second-hand beach rat than fitted, fashion-forward boutique. He glanced towards the water, its proximity one of the reasons he had knocked down Merlin's to build his tower. Still plenty of boats in the marina, but a disproportionate number of pontoons, skiffs, and houseboats. The garish yachts that just yesterday had dominated the docks... only a couple remained.

The disparate sensual cues were deeply troubling for Vern, whose autonomic instinct was to run to his mother. And so he did.

28

VERN VISITS HIS MOTHER AGAIN

Most of the streets in Ulmer Park were indistinguishable from the Ulmer Park where Vern had grown up. Vern had hit the nail quite on the head earlier while riding in the cab from the airport to the Ritz. The historical society in this Queen Palm—call it Queen Palm one million, five hundred thirty-three thousand, two hundred and seventeen, and also call it Sawnichikee, since it had never changed names here—held much more sway than historical societies in other Queen Palms and, as such, its original neighborhoods were astonishingly well-preserved. (Whether this particular Queen Palm/Sawnichikee Historical Society owed its relative vigor to the complete lack of existence of a Vern Bushnell is an intriguing thesis.)

As Vern walked down Osprey Avenue, all of the businesses he once knew still stood. It reminded him of his trip to Prague, how the city center that had escaped bombing in the wars of the 20th century had been preserved, and how wandering those streets felt like walking back in time. Same thing here on Osprey: the pancake place where his mother had taken him on his first day of sixth grade, the newsstand that he had been stealing cigarettes from since he was eleven, the vitamin store, the camera shop, the antiquarian books, on and on. The only noticeable difference was the absence of The Bullet Hole, where Vern's daddy had purchased Vern's first hunting rifle. In its place was a Thai coffee shop. Vern stared at the patrons and their cold brew.

Understanding, if not acceptance, began to rumble deep in his subconscious. He squelched it and walked on, coming up with rational explanation after rational explanation.

When he finally made it to Ohio Street his heart sunk at the sight of his childhood home. It had been painted green. *Green.* With red accents. And the front lawn was covered in statuary. This statuary had no thematic harmony. There were flamingos, naturally. A deer. A virgin Mary. A jockey boy. A giant chrome bowling ball on a pedestal. A few gargoyles. And in the driveway, oh dear god no, a Prius. His mind, saturated with rational explanations and unwilling/unable to deal with what was right in front of him, went immediately to his brother, Bryce. That son of a bitch had gone and sold their childhood home to some kook!

Vern marched to the front door and knocked. He would buy the house back, or threaten litigation, and give Bryce such an earful—

Vern's mother answered the door.

Now, I'd like to interject for just a moment. I don't want you to feel like I'm hitting you over the head with anything. I trust you to catch the subtext. But in this particular instance, I also feel obliged to remind you that a man, no matter how vile and self-centered, has a soft spot for his mother. And we'd all like to think that our mother would be less happy in a world without us. Now, it's all well and good when, within the context of a dysfunctional maternal relationship, a woman tells her son "you ruined my life" or "I wish you'd never been born." This is timelessly human and can be sloughed off. But to experience the unencumbered reality unfold before your very eyes that your mother is, indeed, far happier and healthier in a world where you are and always have been non-existent... there's no spite or resentment in it. It just *is*. And boy oh boy oh boy, that can hurt.

Mary Ann Bushnell wore an intricately embroidered peasant dress that left her willowy arms exposed. Her hair, which had always hidden beneath a crisply-manicured auburn wig, framed her face in naturally flowing gray cascades. Most ghastly of all, in Vern's struggling-to-remain-rational mind, were the worn leather sandals and the bright blue toenails emerging from them.

But there was something else that was harder to discern. Mary Ann Bushnell, that frightened and cautious woman, upon opening her front door to a disheveled and unshaven stranger, did not glare at him with her trademark disdain or address him from a tiny crack twixt door and frame. On the contrary, she opened the door wide with a beaming smile and a look that seemed to say "You. You're alright!"

Vern, for what felt like the eight hundredth time in the past few hours, was speechless.

"Gooood Morning!" his mother said. Even her voice was richer, more resonant, more alive. "You must be a friend of Bryce's."

Vern snapped to.

"That's right, ma'am." A cosmic lie.

"He'll be around any minute. Would you care to come inside?"

Vern said nothing. It came off as avoidance, probably, but he was truly under the spell of Mesmer. He ambled into his childhood home, vaguely hoping to locate himself. But he was nowhere. He was invisible in this home. Family portraits hung on walls and sat on surfaces, spanning the years, reflecting not the slightest trace of him. Anywhere.

And the artwork. It was unduly bohemian. And the whole place stank of sandalwood. There were a few familiar pieces. Recognizable heirlooms. Trinkets from his parents' time in Cambodia. But everything else was foreign and almost seemed to have been picked out with a fierce resolve to offend his sensibilities.

"Would you like a cold drink?"

Vern met his mother's angelic gaze.

"I'm going to have a rosé spritzer," she said. "I could make you one. Or maybe you'd rather have a beer?"

"Thank you. Yes. Beer."

Vern took in more of the bizarro: no fewer than four cats slept on the Boho patchwork sectional, there were books on the shelves instead of Hummel figurines, and Vern was fairly sure that he heard Judy Collins playing softly from the den.

Vern's mother handed him a cold beer. He took a long, quenching pull, then pressed the cold bottle against his forehead.

"You have a lovely home," he said. "How long have you lived here?"

"Oh, shoot, I don't know. At least forty years, I'd say. My husband and I—"

"Bought it sight unseen."

"Yes!"

She loved that story.

"You had to get out of the snow."

"That's right." She smiled. Her eyes crinkled most charmingly. "You're an intuitive, aren't you?"

"I'm a Catholic, ma'am."

"All the same."

"Is your husband... I mean, what does your husband do?"

"My husband passed away several years ago."

Many years before Vern broke his father's heart, the two of them used to go to a magical place called Denner Dogs. The proprietor, Al, was a coronary personified. In thirty years of operation, he had never changed the grease. He'd never washed the grills. Or the floors. Or his hands. Vern's dad would get two chili cheese dogs, a basket of fries, and two Mr. Pibbs to go. And then they'd drive over to the airport and eat their deadly lunches while they watched airplanes take off.

Later on, when Vern's father's heart exploded, some of his crueler associates told Vern that he was probably the one who had killed his dad, but Vern knew it was the Denner Dogs. Anyone who'd ever taken a nutrition class knew it was the Denner Dogs. In communion with the Chesterfields. Did Vern know that he caused his father a great deal of heartache? Undoubtedly. But no one with a real understanding of human anatomy and physiology would assert that the old man's interpersonal dealings with his son had anything to do with his cardiac issues. And here, in this reality, this point was driven home with aplomb. Because here, with no extant Vern, the old man had managed to croak just fine without any help from him.

But the news of his father's passing did not bring on any sense of vindication. He simply felt a gentle constriction, an exquisite feather-brush of loss.

"I'm sorry to hear that," said Vern.

"Well. He had a good long life."

"Yes."

At no point had Mary Ann given any indication that Vern was even remotely familiar to her. The gentle constriction tightened a couple ticks.

"Does Bryce have any brothers or sisters?"

"No, no. One was enough."

Mary Ann crunched an ice cube and then, more out of curiosity than suspicion, said, "You didn't say how you know Bryce."

Vern was spared having to construct another lie by the sound of the front door opening.

"And here he is! I told you any minute. We're in here, Bry!"

And in walked Bryce, carrying a canvas bag full of produce that Vern instinctively knew was entirely organic. Bryce had also changed some. He wore cut-off jean shorts and a fluorescent tank top and brimmed with an air of liberation that struck Vern as distasteful. No trace of the dour, conservative Bryce remained. He glowed.

Apologies, but another momentary interjection. You may be wondering if Bryce's *joie de vivre* had anything to do with not having grown up with a brother named Vern. No one would judge you for making such a logical assumption. Much like the Historical Society being able to flourish without a Vern around Godzilla-stomping city codes. But, you also may be wondering, didn't we just posit that Vern's father's Denner Dog death came on despite the lack of Vern-based stress? Hmmm? What is the nature of cause and effect? Well, once we accept that universes are infinite, perhaps we need to release our simpler ideas of causality and correlation. Back to Bryce.

"They didn't have any watercress, but I picked up some fresh— " He saw Vern sitting on the couch gawking at him. "Oh, hello. I didn't know we had guests."

Vern's shock brought him to his feet.

"Bryce!"

"Yes?"

Vern looked at this marvelously unencumbered man for a blessed beat. "Bryce?!"

"Right both times."

"Bryce, please tell me you know who I am."

Bryce scrutinized him. Coyly. Almost flirtatiously. Then he burst into playful laughter. "Oh my God! Did I meet you on LeBarge?"

Their mother set down her spritzer and clapped her hands. "Oh I love their sunset cruises!"

Vern was nonplussed. "LeBarge? Are you serious?"

"No? You sure it wasn't Freddie Mercury night?"

Bryce smirked and then got down to the serious business of placing how he knew the stranger in his mother's living room.

"I'll admit you look familiar. Are you going to make me guess?"

Vern's dizziness and nausea returned with conviction. "What the hell has gotten into you people?" His legs turned to rubber. The room spun. "What the hell has gotten into *every*thing??" He heard his mother and brother call out as everything went black.

When Vern's eyes fluttered open his mother was pressing a cold washcloth to his forehead. Bryce was daintily mopping up the beer that Vern had spilled when he lost consciousness.

"Mama?"

Mary Ann chuckled sweetly.

"Did he just call you Mama?" asked Bryce.

"He sure did."

"Adorbs!" And they laughed at him.

"You're okay now," she said. "You're probably just overheated."

Vern began to speak but thought better of it. Bryce brought him a glass of ice water.

"I'm sorry that I don't remember who you are. I didn't mean to upset you."

Vern's thoughts stampeded. He looked around the room again. He looked at his mother and his brother in their new incarnations. He sat up, took the ice water, and studied it. As the stampede passed, his ego was left trampled. Whatever was going on, it resisted his attempts to bend it to his will.

"Just to be clear," said Vern, "neither of you has any idea who I am?"

Bryce and Mary Ann looked at each other and then back at Vern. They spoke in unison.

"No."

Vern stood up unsteadily.

"I... I have to go."

Mary Ann placed a hand on his arm. "Easy, sugar. Rest a bit. You're bound to pass out again."

"I'm fine. Thank you. Thank you both. I have to..."

Vern backed his way to the front door and left the house.

29

PORTRAIT OF THE CONGRESSMAN AS
A METAPHYSICAL TRANSIENT

Vern wove through the statuary in his mother's front yard
like a lab rat in a Twilight Zoned maze. He tried to walk,
dignified, but his feet kept bursting into short skittering sprints.
He had to yank on his reins again and again. He aimed for his
favorite boyhood shortcut through an overgrown alley on
Pompano Street and popped out in the heart of a very quiet
downtown Sawnichikee.

His hometown, owing to its distinctive climate, had always
drawn a fair amount of transients and he would often see them
wandering the streets with vague purpose, but he'd never
attempted to fathom where they were headed. Now he began
to realize, being something of a bindlestiff himself, that the urge
to keep moving, even with no destination in mind, was involun-
tary and unavoidable. Like an amputee who still feels his lost
appendage, so does the transient feel a phantom yen to keep
appointments. In this spirit, he headed toward the Starbucks
with full knowledge that he had no means of purchasing
anything.

When he got to the appropriate corner, Starbucks was not

there. In its place was good old Tucker's Sporting Goods, defunct since 1993 in most universes. Vern felt a need to land somewhere. But where was there? He turned in place, still feeling that sharkish compulsion to move, move, move, swim or die. As he swiveled around to the small public park across the street from what should have been the Starbucks, he saw seated on a bench in the shade of a banyan tree the timeless man in the white shirt that had ogled him outside of the Ritz. Vern paced toward him. The man's craggy face curled into an arch smirk.

"Who are you?" demanded Vern.

"I'm Agent D'Angelo."

"*Agent?*"

"Yessir."

D'Angelo sipped from a Starbucks to-go cup. Vern eyed it greedily, clung to his last shreds of pride.

"And do you know who I am?"

"Of course I do, Congressman."

Finally being addressed by his honorific pretty much undid Vern. He spluttered. "Well well so there. Hmmmm. Tell me, Agent. Just tell me what is wrong with everyone else around here??"

D'Angelo patted the space on the bench next to him. "Have a seat, Congressman Bushnell."

Vern crumpled onto the bench. D'Angelo had been briefed. He knew that Vern's capacity for abstraction was limited. But diving right in headlong seemed like the only way to go.

"Congressman, have you heard tell of the multiverse?"

"The... the say what now?"

"Back in 1961, a program was initiated by the United States Government that focused on the possibility of the transference of organic matter between different yet simultaneously existing realities."

Vern stared at D'Angelo. D'Angelo realized that along with abstraction any big words, technical specifications, or quantum anything wouldn't land. He downshifted to pre-school.

"We used wormholes and jazz to blow your mind."

D'Angelo kept talking. Vern kept staring. Nothing made sense to him, but still there seemed to be some subtext to be garnered. Something dark, disturbing, and sinister was being relayed, though the specifics were lost in the serpentine phonemes emitting from the ageless agent's mouth.

When D'Angelo finished speaking, Vern sat for a few moments in silence. Everything caught up with him. His brain rattled to life and his new reality began to form edges and textures in his mind. But just to be sure, he said, "So, I... I'm... what am I?"

"You're still you. A better question would be *where* am I."

"OK then. Where am I?"

"You're in a parallel universe where you have never existed. Here, 'Vern Bushnell' is non-existent. Your history doesn't exist here. Your relationships don't exist here. In a real way, Mr. Bushnell, your slate has been wiped clean. So perhaps 'what am I' is the more apt question. Without our past, what are we indeed?" D'Angelo downed the last of his coffee and dropped the cup into the trash next to the bench as he waited for Vern to respond.

"Well, this won't do!" Vern even had the gumption to smack a fist onto his thigh. "This won't do at all!"

The last thing D'Angelo wanted was for Bushnell to wind himself up into a tantrum. He stood and stretched. "I am sorry, Mr. Bushnell. I know it's a lot to take in. But hey, look, if it makes you feel any better, there's this: if you are as vital a bigshot as you think you are, who knows? You could get called back again. They didn't just off you. That's something."

"Called back? When? How soon? Wait. OFF me??"

D'Angelo had been through this orientation many times. Usually with unsavory characters with inflated senses of their importance. But they typically were conniving or skillful at something, and at the very least passably competent as a mover or shaker. But this Bushnell guy. My god. This whimpering simp was a leading candidate for a Governorship back in their original universe? What was his country coming to? D'Angelo didn't even have the strength to be mad about it, he just felt existential exhaustion. Chop chop, let's get this done and take the weekend.

"Here, Mr. Bushnell. Your new life." D'Angelo dropped into Vern's lap a wallet, a passport, and a leather satchel with travel-sized toiletries. Then he handed down a motel room key. "You're in number eight at the Spanish Village Motor Lodge. There are some clothes in the closet. Your country will pay your weekly rent until you can properly assimilate. There's a debit card in the wallet there, with a little money for incidentals, and a social security card and whatnot. But take it easy. They don't refill the damn thing so budget accordingly and get yourself a job sooner than later."

Vern surveyed his meager worldly belongings. He looked up with the puppiest puppy-dog eyes D'Angelo had ever seen. It was all he could do not to backhand him across the jaw.

"How long?" Vern asked.

"No idea," said D'Angelo. "Maybe a day. Maybe forever. I'll be checking in periodically. You have a nice day now, Mr. Cutler."

As D'Angelo walked away, Vern looked at his passport: "Vernon J. Cutler"

At least they let him keep his first name.

30

VERN CHECKS IN TO THE SPANISH VILLAGE MOTOR LODGE

V ern knew the place. One time when Mia got mad and kicked Vern out of the house, he'd holed up for a few weeks at the Spanish Village. This was many years ago and it had been some time since Vern had personally encountered this level of squalor. Faux wood paneling. Nicotine-stained curtains. The faint smell of sulfur. His first night was fitful as the sounds of cut-rate coitus came at him from both adjoining walls.

Vern was predictably at sea in this baffling reality. Since waking up in the main terminal, observing the inexplicable changes in the landscape, and absorbing the abrupt dissolution of his prestige, Vern had teetered between an assortment of hypotheses. He had first considered the possibility that this was all a bad dream. This hypothesis was supported by the sheer absurdity and backwardness of the civic master plan and the way it seemed to volley twixt some kind of regressive dystopia and pie-eyed progressive paradise. But no amount of pinching could dissolve the illusion.

Another possibility was that this was some brilliantly orchestrated practical joke. But the plausibility of this notion, given the sheer logistics, was even less likely.

That alleged Agent D'Angelo's explanation, though the stuff of second-rate science fiction, seemed to hold the most water. Especially by the time the fourth morning rolled around and Vern awoke, again, in his sad suite at the Spanish Village with no change of status and no fresh towels. But seriously. Come on, now. Parallel universes? Wormholes? Vern just couldn't swallow it. If he just trudged forward, things would go back to how they were. Wouldn't they?

So his third day as Vernon J. Cutler proceeded as the previous two had: disregarding D'Angelo's insistence on austerity and spending the daytime hours and his dwindling savings on hot dogs, warm beer, and questionable bets at the Sawnichikee Kennel Club.

It was a place of considerable solace for him because it seemed to be one of the handful of locales, at least in walking distance, that existed in almost precisely the same form in both this Sawnichikee and his own beloved Queen Palm. The entrance, in both universes, was adorned with the same huge mural of a sinewy Greyhound in mid-race. And the horribly lit interior, in both universes, welcomed the low-lifes and day-drinkers to the cordial asylum where no one judged transience, shiftlessness, or hard luck.

Vern found something meditative in watching the anemic-looking dogs chasing a stuffed rabbit around the track. It soothed the vexing evanescence of his soul. Even when his dog lost, which was far more often than not.

After his shift at the track, Vern would unwind with a few boilermakers at Memories Lounge, another consistent multi-dimensional holdout. Free popcorn provided him the fiber that the dog track cuisine lacked.

This was Vern's routine for the first week or so of his banishment and he was surprised to find that this regiment suited him well enough.

31

VERN'S ENTITLEMENTS LAPSE

Vern blew furiously on the debit card's magnetic strip. He'd already tried licking it and wiping it with his shirt-tail. He'd tried praying over it. Begging it. Cursing at it. Calling it a cocksucker. All to no avail. Each attempt resulted in the same message: "Insufficient Funds."

Vern shoved back the bubbling panic and threw himself a logic Hail Mary: perhaps the ATM at the dog track wasn't routinely serviced. Of course, that was it! So he walked three miles to a credit union and made multiple attempts there at withdrawing funds but was met with similar results. With only seventeen dollars cash left in his coffers, Vern determined that another tack might be called for.

He was still deeply skeptical of D'Angelo's jargon-laden explanation for this bizarre limbo, but he reasoned that, if D'Angelo was speaking any semblance of truth and he was indeed in a parallel universe, then there *must* be another Vern Bushnell circulating about from whom he could siphon funds using his fingerprints or security questions or something. It simply wasn't possible that he didn't exist. D'Angelo had said that to just scare him, to keep him from talking to his parallel self and causing some kind of Star Trek-y, time-travel-y chaos.

He hiked to the public library and waited for an open computer. He sat, cracked his knuckles, and loosed the web browser hounds on "Vern Bushnell, Florida." A millisecond later the screen filled with a handful of hits. Vern smirked. He had outwitted his captors. He'd swipe some cash while avoiding direct contact with "Vern." Both crises averted. He clicked the links.

Fruitless. None of the Vern Bushnells were him. There was an 86-year-old retired plumber and Rotarian in Brooksville, decidedly not Vern and also dead. There was a twelve-year-old wrestling champ in Inverness. A multi-media artist in Key Largo. A detective in Jupiter.

Vern chewed his lip. Maybe, in this universe, he didn't live in Florida! Out-of-state searches turned up plenty of results but none of them lined up with Vern's stats. He sat and stared at the communal computer.

He really... did not... exist here. The spiritual wallop of accepting this truth momentarily distracted him from the pressure of his finances. He re-read the plumber-Rotarian's obituary and wondered what it all meant.

A librarian tapped him on the shoulder. His time was up.

Vern trudged back to the Spanish Village and meekly approached the front desk. The weary innkeeper eyed Vern warily. This guy from room eight had in one short week verbally accosted almost every member of the staff. "You run out of towels again?"

"Listen, man, I got a problem."

"Okay..."

"The fella that pays my rent? I really need to talk to him. It's very important. Do you know how to contact him?"

"You're the guy in number eight, right?"

"Yeah. Vern Bush— Cutler. That's right."

The innkeeper tried not to let his schadenfreude show. At least not too obviously. "Nah. I get a money order every week. That's it."

"Someone brings you a money order?"

"I get it in the mail. Every Thursday. All it says is 'Unit 8.'"

"I can't begin to tell you how important it is that I contact the fella. You got nothing to go on?"

"Sorry, man."

"Well, shit..."

This forced a profound change in Vern's routine. Even his modestly priced pastimes were not fiscally sustainable anymore, so he took to watching a lot of daytime TV and occasionally wandering the streets checking phone booths and vending machines for coins. Technology had rendered this a wholly underwhelming vocation.

Within a couple of days, he was eating Cheerios from a box, drinking water from the tap, watching *The Price is Right* in his unlaundered undies. His last few coins sat on the nightstand, next to the phone, which suddenly rang as a lady screeched in tormented joy as her chip plinko'd. It was the front desk.

"I'm very sorry, sir, but you must vacate."

"What??"

"Your weekly check did not arrive yesterday. You're paid through 10 am tomorrow."

"But—"

"You have a nice day, now." Click.

Vern replaced the receiver, turned off the TV, pulled on some clothes, and went a-wandering. Again, no destination in mind, just a vague plan to luck into some money. As he waited for a traffic light to change and the "walk" sign to flash, he realized he was still munching Cheerios. He looked around, embarrassed, and stuffed the almost empty box into the corner trash.

Traffic going that-a-way stopped. Traffic going this-a-way started. The sign blinked "walk."

Vern walked, head down, block after block, lamenting his piss-poor fortune. A giant SUV honked and almost clipped him. He leaped back a step but didn't even have the energy to spew a curse much less flip a bird. But that SUV had given Vern a gift. Now that his eyes were up, he saw a familiar and oddly comforting sign: Johnny's Car Wash.

A warming sense of recognition caused a rush of endorphins and a glimmer of hope. Vern's talents—glad-handing, bullying, blackmailing, double-talking—were doing little to help him as Vern Cutler the Nobody. But back in the day... before the Sneeds... Vern had what he now realized was a marketable gift. He was a supremely gifted car washer.

Johnny's was clearly understaffed as a line of cars waited for a single detailer to get to them. Opportunity knocked. Vern answered. He tucked his shirt in, feebly fixed his hair, and headed into the waiting area. An employment application was already sitting on the desk, bathed in a shaft of sunlight that had squeezed through the shades, and the owner happened to be there. Vern sucked in a breath... he knew the owner from his universe. This was Johnny's nephew, who Vern had tormented when they worked the line together as teens. But Johnny's nephew in this universe didn't know Vern or remember any torment and in fact was deeply grateful for an applicant. Vern filled out the application lickety-split. Johnny's nephew asked a few cursory questions, promptly retreated to the back office, and returned with a crisp "Johnny's" t-shirt which he gave to Vern along with a handshake that damn near dispersed his carpals. Vern Cutler née Bushnell was gainfully employed.

32

THE SNEEDS' PLAN B

L est we forget, back in our universe, life went on without Vern Bushnell to push around. The Sneeds, you gotta hand it to them, had a superhuman sort of pragmatism. Less than a week since the Bushnell debacle, they were right back in the saddle. True, they now regretted the costly preening they'd given Vern Bushnell. His abrupt disappearance had not only upended the primary but also resulted in the Pontus Supreme B-15 fallout landing a bit too close to them for comfort. But they'd bobbed and weaved like champs and emerged relatively unscathed. They put their disappointment behind them and moved on. There was, after all, still time to futz with the gears of power.

The new beneficiary of their sociopathy was mean old Pat Lueke. They had lost a valuable megaphone in Vern, and despite the improbability of commandeering a viable candidate, they couldn't allow the election cycle to be a complete wash. They needed to engage a pliable frontman, but fast, lest their painstakingly established agitprop slip from the collective unconscious. And Pat Lueke was the best they could come up with on such short notice. To make the old bastard feel extra special, the Sneeds had even deigned to visit him in his office to make the pitch.

Lueke's aide led the Sneeds into Pat's office. Sandy gazed on the pink, doddery bruiser. He looked old. He looked deranged. His suit fit him like a potato sack. Sandy Sneed mentally shuffled through his carefully curated Rolodex of acceptable human greetings and came up with, "There's old Pat!"

"Sandy! Malcolm! Come on in. Sit down, please." Lueke had been waiting for this day since the late '70s. The money cats always seemed to bankroll candidates with more polish, and polish was never Lueke's thing. But he knew his day would eventually come because he'd inherited from his male ancestors such remarkable, demented tenacity.

Malcolm Sneed took in the artifacts adorning Lueke's office walls. A mounted marlin. Awkward family photos. A picture of Lueke with Sylvester Stallone. A portrait of Teddy Roosevelt. Any number of plaques from dubious social organizations.

The Sneeds knew too well that Pat Lueke had ample baggage. But, symbolically speaking, the move was brilliant. He was, truly, the only living link to the last administration which had managed to finish things out without making the party look ineffectual and obsolete. Thirty long years ago he had served as communications director for the bold and revered and historically revised President Lipton.

Malcolm spotted another relic on Lueke's wall that drove this point home: a picture from the early '80s of a manic young Lueke shaking hands in the Oval Office with a visibly uncomfortable Lipton. It was fairly clear, even then, that Lueke was a loose cannon. And as he advanced in his public service his confidence in his deranged notions of democracy engorged and calcified. Everyone suspected that he had a drinking problem but he never touched the stuff. He was just naturally mean and crazy. But, on the upside, his mere presence kept the dialogue reminiscent of happier times.

Malcolm glanced at his brother. Yep. This was the best they had. He took a breath and plunged. "Pat. We're changing things up a little bit. You feeling plucky?"

Lueke beamed. Who did they think they were talking to? He was nothing if not plucky. "My friends," said Pat Lueke, "I am honored."

33

THEM STEADILY DEPRESSIN', LOW DOWN MIND MESSIN', WORKING AT THE CAR WASH BLUES

A lot of people are under the impression that art is absent in menial labor. Anyone can apply a coat of wax to a Buick, yes. But an eye for luster, an appreciation for the nuance of the finish, a keen intuition for the proportion of gloss to matte based on the character and sensibility of an automobile's design? That can only serve to elevate the vocation.

Because to an artist, there's no hierarchical curve between a Saab and a Pontiac, but there is a distinctive temperament in either. An Impala and a Spyder have, intrinsically, the same rights to a thorough detailing, but an artist knows that the Impala is inherently taciturn and modest whilst the Spyder has more temerity. The degree of shine should, naturally, reflect this heterogeneity. The professional understands the need for harmonic unity between engineered design and after-factory maquillage. And that is just the insight that Vern possessed. He hadn't lost his skill. He was still, after all these years, a formidable car washer.

Indeed, Vern's superiority of craft was apparent to the extent that after only a week on the job he had earned the full confidence of the proprietor. Johnny's nephew couldn't believe his luck. He happily gifted Vern three fresh t-shirts to save his needing to do laundry every night. In no time at all, a handful of discerning patrons were requesting Vern in particular.

Throughout Vern's rapid rise to prominence in his field, D'Angelo had been in absentia. At first, Vern had taken this as a personal affront. At regular intervals, he'd find himself cursing D'Angelo and calling him incompetent behind his back. But as time went on Vern's tightened dendrites uncoiled. He began to see nuances in humanity the way he did in cars. So his curses gave way to reasoning and grace. Most likely D'Angelo was tending to countless other people in countless other universes. Possibly even countless other Verns in countless other universes! So Vern decided to forgive D'Angelo for halting the rent payments, especially since he now was writing that weekly check just fine. D'Angelo freezing the handout had forced Vern to rediscover his agency and self-reliance, right? And it's not like D'Angelo hadn't warned him. Might as well take it easy on the old guy.

Vern discovered that he was feeling good if a little alone. He had yet to make any real friends, but he felt more grounded, more himself, more... alive?... than he had in a very, very long time. Not merely happy. But content. Useful.

All that matters is mattering.

It was in such a mindset one fine morning that Vern brilliantly applied a luscious coat of Turtle Wax to a Nissan Altima. He was so lost in his work, caught up in the angles of the side panel and the variations in the paint, that he didn't even notice he had drawn a crowd. Patrons and co-workers alike marveled at his precision and efficiency. Without moving fast, he finished quickly. As he nonchalantly flicked his rag with one hand while closing the wax with the other, his audience burst into spontaneous applause. This completely unlooked-for adulation finally brought his attention back to the present. He smiled shyly, gave a little bow, and accepted a vigorous handshake and hefty tip from the Altima's owner.

As he took his well-earned respite on the employee bench, guzzling Gatorade and receiving high-fives, his gaze wandered across the Trail. He was fast becoming able to tell the time of day by the denizens of the bus stop. Judging by the presence of the middle-aged gentleman with the Publix polo he figured it must be around 11:30. He was, as usual, joined by the little old lady with giant sunglasses and a canvas bag full of library books. And, smoking a long cigarette at a polite distance from the others, a tall black man whose tailored suit was always sharp and always wholly unsuitable for the Florida heat. Today's collective was about to be joined by another Sawnichi-keeite whose presence would disrupt the freshly established order of Vern's new existence.

A slim, 50ish woman in Earth Mother garb and an Annie Hall hat jogged toward the stop as the bus approached. She was of striking contrast to the usual suspects in that, even in her rush, she seemed to defy concern and trot an inch or two off the ground. She greeted the others warmly as she rifled through her beaded purse for bus fare. She was an exquisite paradox to the assembly... ethereal but palpable, delicate but rugged, spectral but inescapably human.

I know, I know, I know. You're way ahead of me. This was Mia. Of course it was. But far removed from the sad, sedated quiddity of her ivory tower back in our universe, this Mia was fresh and effervescent and vivacious.

"Mia...?" Vern asked himself.

"Mia," he answered.

"MIA!" he cried out.

Seeing her cracked Vern open. His blood hummed. His nerves buzzed. His Gatorade spilled as he shot to his feet.

The bus pulled up to the stop. Vern dropped his polishing rag and ran to the curb, somehow refraining from running headlong into oncoming traffic.

"MIA!" he called again.

When the bus pulled away from the stop, she was gone.

But now Vern had clarity. He knew why everything had conspired to bring him here. He finished his shift in a blissed-out haze, which rather than distracting him from his job only elevated his work to the level of the sublime. His pockets bulged with incredulous tips.

That evening after work Vern spent his beer money at Alberti's Barber Shop on Main Street. He even sprang for a shave. When he got back to his suite at the Spanish Village he went right for the phone book in the nightstand and flipped through the pages. When he found no entries for Mia under her maiden name, Vern became filled with the dreadful notion that, in his absence, she had married someone else. Then he realized this was a minor point, given their cosmic connection. He'd doubtless be able to wrest her away from whatever undeserving clod had won her. But her absence from the phone book would make the process more arduous than he'd expected.

No matter. He resolved to stay shaven and presentable. He bought a wrinkle-free collared shirt to keep with him at the car wash so he could make a dashing escape the next time she appeared. And he waited, a fantastical sense of purpose motivating his every move. He began to wrangle with his sense of entrepreneurship, ascertaining a manner by which he could elevate himself enough to carve out a comfortable life for them once reunited. Certainly not as opulent as their life in Queen Palm. But being on the line at the car wash wouldn't do long-term, no sir. Maybe Johnny's nephew would consider franchising, and Vern could lead the expansion of the empire?

Mia didn't appear the next day. Or the next. Vern did not

despair. He took a lunch with Johnny's nephew and laid some groundwork. He cranked out wash-wax-detailing jobs on par with Picassos and Monets. He kept his jaw stubble-free and his hair washed and combed.

And on the third day, with the bus a mere five blocks away, she appeared. Vern tore off his Johnny's T, grabbed his "church shirt," and darted across the Trail, dodging a few cars Frogger-style and reaching the bus just before the doors closed.

After paying his fare, Vern turned and took a gander at his seating options. Mia was four rows back reading a John D. McDonald novel and not giving him a second look. He contemplated sitting next to her but figured that might creep her out. After all, he thought, she doesn't know me yet. Better to do recon. He walked past her row and sat two seats behind her. A respectable distance but one from which he could smell her perfume. Gardenias. So Mia.

The bus headed past downtown and onto Gulfstream Avenue. Vern hadn't yet familiarized himself with public transportation and had no idea what Mia's destination might be. He also didn't know how Johnny would react to his abrupt departure, mid-way through servicing a Grand Cherokee, especially considering their recent blue sky convo. He found he didn't want to lie to his boss, and that was a strange bit of self-realization, but he also knew his unique acumen and well-received ambition would give him some wiggle room. The reprimand would probably result in some mild humiliation but would be oh so worth it.

The bus continued to the causeway and over the bay, past Pelican Cove and into the bougie shopping district bordering the public beach. Vern was taken aback by the continued absence of condominium buildings, but it wasn't affecting his mood like it had when he'd first arrived. The views, he had to admit, were far improved. He had taken in quite a few spectacular sunsets, something he had neglected to do back in Queen Palm.

The bus stopped and Vern perked up. The man in the Publix shirt got off the bus at Chiles Street. The old lady with the library books got off a few stops closer to the beach. The man in the suit got off in front of the Bilmar Resort and immediately lit a cigarette.

A few minutes later Mia closed her book and gracefully reached above her head and pulled the cord for her stop. Vern looked out the window and couldn't help but chuckle at the full-circleness of it all. The bus gently halted in front of the Azure Tides, sans demolition crews and protestors. No longer flanked by garish development, the Azure Tides, in its gorgeous rusticity, instead shared its borders with a few vacation cottages and an unpretentious mid-century hotel.

In order to remain unobtrusive, Vern stayed on the bus after Mia got off. He rode it to the next stop and doubled back on foot.

34

VERN IS AFFORDED THE
OPPORTUNITY TO ANONYMOUSLY HIT
ON HIS WIFE

Vern opened the heavy cypress door to the Azure Tides, which allowed a burst of sunlight to flashbulb the dark watering hole. A few of the patrons squinted at him with annoyance. The door swung shut behind him and it took a few seconds for his eyes to adjust to the ambiance. He hadn't been inside the place since the days that such an activity required a fake ID. It was exactly as he remembered it. Indescribably seedy, but harmless. Even cozy. The bar was polished driftwood and the stools were tattered red vinyl. Cigarette smoke filtered the scant light sources, creating the sort of effect that old soap operas had used to connote a dream sequence.

Mia held court behind the bar with effortless generosity and skillful joy. It was clear she had become the beating heart of the joint. Devoid of her trademark pathos, she glowed like Aphrodite, but in a warm and approachable way. No stern distance separated this queen from her people. The relationship between her, the bar, and the patrons was beautifully symbiotic. Vern watched as she mixed a margarita from scratch and playfully placed it in front of a smitten geriatric.

Vern approached. His heart beat a beguine in his chest and all his carefully rehearsed opening lines flew clean out of his head.

"Heya," said Mia.

His faculties temporarily suspended, Vern just stared. She waited, her patience refined by years of dealing with all the wonderfully odd personalities that tumbled down the continent into Florida's funnel. After the appropriate number of beats, long enough not to rush him but also not so long as to make it awkward for all involved parties, Mia asked, "Thirsty?"

Vern had yet to recover. He was utterly gobsmacked. So he just nodded.

"What can I get you?"

As Mia magicked a coaster into existence before him, Vern pondered her question. "What can I get you?" It was such an *excellent* question. Erudite and probing. Vern was certain that his answer would reveal everything about him, and that was worrisome. Naturally, a bourbon and soda was what he wanted. And if Mia knew him, she wouldn't have to ask. But this Mia was not privy to Vern's drink of choice. So this drink order was the occasion that would set into motion the miraculous second-take in the tale of Vern and Mia, and so he felt compelled to step outside the box and order something exotic.

"Ummm. Long Island Iced Tea?"

An expression of teasing scorn crossed Mia's face.

"I'm sorry," she said, "I don't serve those to men over twenty-five."

"What?"

"I'm kidding, friend." She smiled. Vern's legs jellified. Thankfully he was next to a stool and managed to land on it. "Long Island it is."

She moved to the rail and reached for the Triple Sec. And Vern knew he had way way WAY overthought it.

"You know what? Just make it a bourbon and soda."

Mia's smile brightened. Vern's stomach cartwheeled.

"That's more like it," she said. "Figured you for a bourbon fellow."

She poured with surgical precision, wielded the soda gun like Annie Oakley, and set the drink in front of him. "And a very happy Thursday afternoon to you, friend."

Vern decided to be bold. He held up his perfect drink and cheers'd her. "It's Vern."

She cheers'd back with her working glass of water. "Well met, Vern."

"Thank you. Mia."

His prescience zipped by unnoticed. He took a sip and assayed again.

"Hey, did you go Sawnichikee High?"

"Sure did."

"I thought you looked familiar."

"You too?"

"Nah. I went to Riverview. But I think we might have gone to some of the same parties."

"Probably. I was at all of them."

"It *is* Mia, right?"

"Yep, good memory. Would you like to start a tab?"

"No. I'll pay as I go." He handed her a crisp twenty that the driver of a Bentley had tipped him that morning. She turned away to the register. He took a gigantic fortifying swallow, almost to the point of choking and spluttering. This was not in any way going the way he had imagined it would. This was *hard*. And freakishly scary. The iced bourbon burned down his throat. He hadn't had to be authentic in a conversation for years. And here he was, a small-talk prospect barely good enough to crack double-A taking flailing swings at major league chit-chat with everything on the line.

As Mia turned back with his change, he took another Mighty Casey cut. "I've been away for a while. Place sure has changed."

She snorted. Even her *snort* made his heart constrict.

"Sawnichikee? You kidding? Place is a goddam time warp."

She had no idea how right she was.

"Where'd you go off to?" she asked. All-Star small-talker.

"Oh... here and there," he answered. End of the bench scrub.

"What'd you come back for?"

He wanted to tell her everything right then and there and get it over with. And she'd believe every insane word and reach for him. And he'd take her in his arms and tell her he'd do better this time. Instead...

"I, um, well my mama's sick."

"Oh, I'm sorry." Her commiseration was of the professional barkeep's kind, sincere without giving anything away.

"Yeah, thanks."

Sunlight burst again as a couple of seasoned day-drunks came in and flagged Mia down.

"Afternoon, Friends! 'Scuse me, Vern." Mia wiped her hands on a bar rag and went to greet the newcomers.

Vern watched her open up a few bottles of High Life and hand them across the bar. She laughed at something the day-drunks said. Vern felt his opportunity at making the striking first impression slipping away. He looked around, groping for a sign, a signal, a clue.

A jukebox stood sentinel in the corner. Inspiration struck. If the old machine had the right song...

Vern beelined to the jukebox and scrolled through the selections. Nothing digital here, the antiquated arms flipped actual *records* back and forth. He searched and searched. He felt sweat on his forehead. It had to be here, it just had to.

THERE.

He fed the machine a quarter (yes, it still took quarters, no debit cards with magic chips here) and pushed a few translucent plastic buttons. The music began. A simple 4/4 pocket of soft-rock drums and bass issued forth. Some melody-teasing synth joined for the first few bars, then a shy electric guitar plucked its way into the mix.

Vern looked back to the bar and sure enough, Mia had frozen in place. Her eyes lighthoused his way just as the iconic, late-70s/early-80s, microphone-dependent, thin tenor squeezed out his first note, heralding the arrival of harmonized call and response.

> (*Sunrise*) *There's a new sun arisin'*
> (*In your eyes*) *I can see a new horizon*
> (*Realize*) *That will keep me realizin'*
> *You're the biggest part of me*

"Are you kidding me, friend?"
Vern moved back to the bar.
"This... is my favorite song ever," she said.
"I know," he thought. "Oh yeah?" he said.
"Ambrooooosia," she cooed.
"Food of the gods," he replied. She snort-grinned. Vern fist-pumped under the bar. There we go! Solid double up the middle. Now we're on.

The tightly meshed Ambrosians headed toward their first chorus. Mia shook her head.

"Oh my god, this takes me back."

They listened in silence. Mia closed her eyes and starting singing along lightly. Vern watched her, aching to join in, but his croaking would surely ruin the spell being cast.

Well, make a wish, baby
And I will make it come true
Make a list baby, of the things I'll do for you
Ain't no risk in lettin' my love rain down on you
So we can wash away the past so that we may
start anew

Vern recalled with exquisite clarity their first night, in Tina, by the water, under the moon, with Ambrosia serenading their initial kiss. "It doesn't seem that long ago..."

"No. But it was."

It was a glorious rekindling until Vern saw it: the ring. Fourth finger. Left hand. And it struck him that this Mia in front of him did not share with him the same memories of this song. There was no past for her to wash away. Only he was in a position to start anew. Somehow, miraculously, in this universe, Mia still loved this song, but not for the same reasons. Perhaps she loved it because of the man or woman symbolized by that motherfucking ring on her finger!

All could not be lost. Vern was nothing if not deluded. He waited for the next verse to land...

(Love flows) Gettin' better as we're older
(All I know) All I wanna do is hold her
She's the life that breathes in me

... then pressed his advantage.

"Did your, uh, husband go to Sawnichickee High?"

Her eyes snapped open. "My husband?"

"Oh, I... I saw the ring and I thought..."

"Oh." She gave him a look. "I just wear it so men won't hit on me."

Vern obliviously plowed on. "You're not, um, spoken for?"

She gave him the look again, temperature turned up. "No."

Vern somehow remained impervious to all the obvious signals radiating from Mia's countenance. He grinned. "Remarkable…"

Mia snorted a third time, and with such supreme annoyance that even Vern couldn't miss it. "No one speaks for me, friend. You want another bourbon?"

Vern blinked. The song still played, but no spell lingered in the hazy air. He was saved by Mia's vocation, thankfully, when a pair of middle-aged bar regulars, preceded by another unforgiving blast of sunshine, came in the front door and bellied up to the bar.

"Mr. and Mrs. Overall! How was Niagara?" She left Vern drinkless and meandered over to the Overalls, placing coasters in front of them and getting to work on their drinks. Vern observed the interaction. There was nothing servile in her engagement. Genuine humanity seemed to motivate her through every step of the exchange. She poured heavy, smiled warmly, seemed actually eager to look at their vacation pictures. Mrs. Overall did the bulk of the talking, which there was a lot of, and Mia's eyes never once wandered. What would've been, to most, a painfully dry conversation with an unremarkable pair of Caucasians about a fairly rote vacation experience, was treated by Mia as a thoroughly fascinating dispatch from an exotic land as recounted by returning heroes. For their part, Mr. and Mrs. Overall seemed grateful to bask in Mia's glowing assessment of them and their stories. How wonderful it must have felt to be familiars, to be recognized, to be seen and heard and approved of with such intensity.

Vern remembered this altruistic virtuosity in her. And if this universe was any indication, Mia's spiritual magnanimity was a consistent fixture in every conceivable timeline. Sure, in Queen Palm, where Vern Bushnell ran roughshod over anything pure, Mia's divinity had been ruefully muted. But here, in Sawnichickee, Vern was reminded of the buoyant, beautiful quintessence that had once moved those aged Teamsters to flap their arms in unison and moved him to a love so supreme that it continued to exist even when his existence was nebulous.

Vern had never intended to push this spectacular personage to the brink. He had never set out to take her for granted or sap her brio or reduce her magic to the realm of the mundane and maudlin. But the stark contrast between the Mia he'd left behind and this Mia was writ large, even for an insensate like Vern. He finally came round to a verity that had festered just under his radar for so many years: He was culpable.

And even worse, he had started his second chance by doing the same damn thing again. Hell, it wasn't even a second chance. He was the one who didn't belong here. Why assume this Mia would even need or want a so-called second chance? And why the hell would she want it with him? He had work to do. He had to remember who he was before he became who he thought he should be. She had fallen in love with Vern before all the money and power and condos. Who had he been before all of that? And was he salvageable? It would be wrong, oh so wrong, to ask her to save him or reclaim him. He had to bring something to the table. And right now it felt like his pockets were empty. He would have to return when he'd regained a more robustly favorable self-assessment. He put a 105% gratuity on the driftwood and quietly left the bar. He didn't even look back.

And so he missed the flickering glance that Mia shot at his retreating form.

35

VERN VISITS HIS MOTHER A
THIRD TIME

That weekend, Vern, armed with carnations wrapped in plastic, returned to the green house in Ulmer Park and knocked on the front door. His mother, Mary Ann, answered the door.

"Well, hello there, Vern! Looks like the last few weeks have been pretty good to you."

Vern extended the flowers to her.

"This is way overdue. I just wanted to thank you for taking care of me."

"Well, aren't you sweet. I should put these in some water. Would you like to come in?"

"Okay."

Vern followed her inside. Mary Ann moved toward the kitchen.

"I might have a beer in there, if you'd like."

"If you've got one."

"Make yourself comfortable. Won't be a minute." She shuffled out of the room.

Vern returned to the photographs hanging on the walls and

crowding the mantle. So much was familiar to him. There... the house on Clippert Street in Dearborn Heights where he'd spent the first chapter of his life. In the photograph, the Bushnells stood in front of the house in church clothes. It was identical to the framed photo that had hung in Queen Palm: Artie and Mary Ann, young and suburban, baby Bryce cradled in Mary Ann's arms, Artie's Fairlane in the driveway. The only thing missing from the picture was Vern. In most other universes he would've been standing in front of his father looking petulant, his father's meaty hands on his shoulders holding him in place for the purposes of posing.

He was especially taken in by a picture of Artie and Mary Ann from the OLD old days. They were so young. They appeared to be on some sort of boardwalk. The beach was in the background and Artie, in a military uniform, was holding a bag of popcorn. Mary Ann's head was thrown back and her mouth was wide open, apparently caught in a hearty guffaw. Artie was smiling, almost smug. He had clearly said something amusing and the picture was taken in the ensuing milliseconds. His parents were never particularly dour but the couple captured by that camera on that boardwalk on that day were as far removed from Vern's concept of his folks as could be. Vern again chewed on the gristle of blame. He couldn't quite swallow it, but it did feed into his uncommon introspection. Like Artie, he had once been a dashing cut-up. Like Mary Ann, Mia had once been irrepressibly good-humored. Was Vern's absence an overall positive for his parents? For his first and only love?

Vern picked up a framed portrait of Artie. This was another one that existed in both universes. He remembered it well. It had been shot by a professional photographer when Artie won a sales contest at the dealership. He was reasonably weathered in this picture but still incredibly sentient. Vern saw something though in this iteration of the picture that he didn't remember from before and it wasn't something he could put words to. His pops had smile lines, graying hair, a furrowed brow, but underneath it all was the innocent pride of a kid who'd just won a spelling bee. Many times throughout his checkered adulthood Vern had been called a "Man Child" by some adversary or another. Now Vern thought, "Aren't we all?"

"That's my husband, Artie." Mary Ann handed Vern a bottle of cold beer. "Almost fifty years we were together, Artie and I."

"That's quite a record."

"Well, people stuck together."

"Must take a lot of compromise. To keep a thing going that long without killing each other."

"You ever been married?"

Vern supposed that his Queen Palm credentials permitted him to answer in the affirmative. "Yeah."

"Did your parents approve?" Mary Ann asked. Even for Vern, this was getting awfully meta. But he had come on this visit intentionally, seeking wisdom or insight or something that could help him track down himself. Part of him wondered if this Mary Ann might, with enough conversation and vulnerability, recognize him. Shouldn't a mother sense her son, even across dimensional boundaries? Wasn't his genetic code hardwired into her as well?

"Yes, actually, my mother approved big-time. Dad not so much. But on the day of, pretty much everyone in the church had high hopes. Especially me."

"And let me guess," Mary Ann said as they sat on the couch. "You pledged to yourself that you and your beloved would never ever ever find yourselves as dull and indifferent as your parents were."

Vern was taken aback. "Um. Yeah."

Mary Ann sighed. "No one ever sees their parents as people. Artie and I were the same. We told each other over and over that we would never lapse into complacency like our parents did. My parents lasted to the end, as did Artie's, but both, it turned out, were rotted from the inside with resentment."

Vern had never actually heard the stories of his grandparents' marriages. So he did something he was horrible at back in his home universe, something that he realized he used to do a lot more of, especially with Mia.

He shut up and listened.

Mary Ann was studying her iced tea. "Oh, Vern. Words get said. Promises get broken. The rituals you build with your sweetie get disbanded for God only knows what reason. And at first, you think these trespasses are unique to you, but you come to realize it's utterly, absolutely normal. Boring even. Marriages are meant to fall into decay. That's just what time does. Even though you know you still love 'em, and that they love you. You ever cheat on her?"

Oh, Vern had had plenty of opportunity. One doesn't rise in the political ranks without learning just how potent a musk power truly is. But say this for our protagonist: he'd never crossed that particular line, even if his motivation was driven more by an instinctive avoidance of potential scandal than abject fealty. As Vern grappled with the intricacies of his integrity, he shook his head.

"No. Never."

"Good for you, Vern. Why make it harder than it has to be?" She put down her tea and picked up the portrait Vern had looked at earlier. "Artie was a good man. Always provided. Never laid a finger on me, rarely said an unkind word. But there was, and I suppose I was guilty too, as I suppose we all were in those days... Love was something to be marked off on a checklist. Like our friends, we rushed into it. Not to say it wouldn't have happened eventually anyway. But at a certain point, despite all the romance, the union itself was just the way of things."

Vern was captivated. He studied his mother studying his father. "You didn't love him?"

"Sure, I loved him. You can't help but love someone you willfully share a space with for that long. You inure. Their peccadilloes are like sofa cushions. And you get cozy. And you get a paunch and little hairs start to grow in their ears. Even their smell or their gas or the way they clear their sinuses becomes endearing and comforting."

She closed her eyes and her lids fluttered in remembrance. "And yet, by heaven, I think my love as rare as any she belied with false compare."

"Shakespeare."

"Sonnet 130. Yes. You know it?"

"Nah. But I know you like him."

"And how would you know something like that?" Mary Ann asked, teasing but with the merest hint of odd suspicion. Vern cursed himself inwardly. Had to tread lightly here. But he had an easy out. He pointed at the bookshelf.

"Well, you've only got like four different Complete Works over there."

Mary Ann chuckled, the suspicion squashed before it had taken a second breath. "I do indeed. I like to compare quartos and folios."

"Sure, yeah." Vern had no idea what she was talking about. He sipped his beer.

Mary Ann set down the portrait and picked at the fringe on a decorative pillow. "Shakespeare didn't always extol the virtues of prosaic love, you know. But it comes in handy when you've settled down and the vapors aren't so vivid as they once

155

were. When love is no longer a 'smoke made from the fume of sighs'—he said that too—then what you have is far less exciting but considerably more real."

Vern wondered to himself why he'd never had this sort of conversation with his mother before. Back in Queen Palm this woman was too far gone to deliver gentle wisdom. But even when she'd been sharp, the idea of engaging in this sort of exchange would've been unthinkable. That sort of access? That brand of honesty? Never. But Vern, in his slowly broadening actualization, realized that it wasn't owing to a lack of maternal generosity. It was simply because Vern never would've sat still long enough to accept it.

"Were we 'star crossed'?" Mary Ann asked no one in particular. "Who knows? Who knows? The only way to know for sure, I suppose, is to never give over in the first place and see how that feels. But that's assuming a level of prescience that eludes me. Artie has shuffled off this mortal coil, so he probably knows, but he's yet to come back to me with a report. Would you like another beer?"

"I really, really would, Mary Ann. Thank you."

"Anytime, Vern. You're always most welcome."

She stood. Vern handed over his empty. As she got to the doorway he compulsively asked, "What if your slate was wiped clean, Mary Ann? Who would you choose to be?"

Mary Ann stopped. Looked at him in such a way that he felt x-rayed. He held his breath.

"If my slate were wiped clean, would I still possess the requisite earned experience to make productive changes?"

"Let's say yes. Let's say you would know then what you know now."

"Well, Vern, of course I'd hope that my life and my self were compelling enough to warrant not making any changes. I also wouldn't want to do anything that would snap Bryce out of existence. But I also think... we aren't the only ones who write on our slate. You may choose who to give your chalk to now and again, but what they choose to write? Well now. You can't control that, can you?"

She exited to the kitchen. Vern sat with his jaw on the floor and his mind blown.

36

THE CONTINUED COURTSHIP OF MIA BUSHNELL NÉE GAUDET

V ern spent the next few days interrogating his reflection in every car he detailed. When not working he wandered the city and studied it with the same intention he had given his mother's photographs. He started looking for a room to let or even a small apartment or carriage house.

On Wednesday afternoon he asked if he could have off the next several Thursdays. He offered to train up the other line workers on his breaks, to make up for his transgression the previous week. Johnny's nephew gladly agreed.

Thursday. Early afternoon. The bus. The causeway. The Azure Tides. The burst of sunlight as he opened the door.

Mia looked up from behind the bar. "Well hello there, Friend. Was wondering if you'd wander back."

"Not all who wander are lost," he replied sagely.

She snorted. "You see that on a T-shirt?"

He chuckled and tapped his finger on his nose. "Right on one."

He bellied up. She poured a bourbon and soda without asking. Vern, his senses far less fogged by shock and entitlement, noted with pleasure that she remembered his drink, but he didn't let it go to his head. He settled in. He was in no rush. He watched her work. Asked her questions. Listened to her answers. Played the occasional song on the jukebox. Wiled away the day. Soaked up his third bourbon with some surprisingly good fried food. Whenever Mia wasn't engaging him in chitchat—which seemed to get more and more frequent—he took in the other patrons, developed a rooting interest in the cornhole tournament being televised on the cable sports channel, and relished simply being near her.

As the sun was setting he left another large tip and got up to leave. Mia pressed pause on a drink order at the other end of the bar and hurried over.

"Not even a fare-thee-well, Friend?"

"Sorry, Mia, you looked busy. I'll be back."

"I know you will. Have a good one, Vern."

Hearing his name drop from her lips was everything. But again, he let it lie. He just gave her a lopsided grin, tipped an invisible hat, and said, "Back to wandering."

"Don't get lost."

"No way no how."

The next several Thursdays unspooled in similar fashion. Mia began to wonder at his seeming perceptiveness. He'd occasionally finish her sentences, but not presumptively or creepily, and his way of speaking was such that she found herself even finishing his. And my god did he have a knack for artfully choosing song after song on the jukebox that rendered her foggy with nostalgia. Slightly unsettling but equally alluring to her was the fact that Vern, when he smiled at her, seemed to know her. She got hit on by guys all the time, and in their eyes she always saw how she was just a reflection of their ego and desire. But in Vern's eyes, she got the distinct impression of seeing herself.

Finally, on the fifth Thursday, two bourbons in, as they both laughed at something one of them had said, he did it.

"What time do you get off?" Vern asked.

Mia could tell he was petrified. "Pardon?"

"I'd like to buy you a grouper sandwich. You in?"

Mia rubbed her rag on a single spot on the bar.

"Oh, Vern. I knew you'd eventually do this."

She saw him deflate then rally.

"Whaddya mean, Mia? You think I come around here only to see you?" He tried to chuckle. It came out a squeezed giggle.

She patted his hand. "I know you do." She went back to rubbing that spot on the bar. "And, honestly, I'm glad you do. Come around, I mean. I've been enjoying our Thursdays."

"So then...?"

"But I was hoping you wouldn't ask so I wouldn't have to say no."

"You *have* to?"

"Yeah."

Vern didn't press. She rubbed that spot on the bar. She sensed him struggling, sensed him trying to find the magic words, trying to figure her out. But then, to her ever-living amazement, he simply said...

"OK."

She stopped rubbing.

"OK?"

"Yeah. OK. If you have to, then you have to. I can't promise I won't ask you again sometime, but..." He shrugged.

"Vern. Thank you. And I want you to know it's—."

"—it's not you, it's me."

She grinned, a bit shy. "It really isn't. Or, I mean, it really is."

"The ultimate cliché, but I believe you."

She rubbed the spot on the bar. He wiped some condensation from his glass. Then he cleared his throat.

"Do you mind if I ask what it is, then? Only if you want to talk about it."

"It's hard to explain."

"I'm a pretty sharp guy. At least my mama always told me so."

It wasn't a good joke. Wasn't even delivered that well. But it was an excuse for them both to laugh a little and let the awkwardness dissipate. Mia put the rag down and granted Vern the luxury of eye contact.

"I'm not dating *anyone* right now. On the advice of my spiritual advisor."

Vern cocked his head. Mia continued.

"My spiritual advisor says that I have a hard time protecting my heart."

"Your spiritual advisor?"

"Yeah. Sheila."

"Sheila."

"Yes."

Mia had to go take care of a couple patrons. Vern watched a commercial for protein powder and a teaser for the evening news. Mia returned.

"So, ok. What's a spiritual advisor do?" Vern asked.

Mia scanned his tone for snark or mockery or belittlement. All clear. He was sincerely asking. Will wonders never cease?

"Sheila helps me access my strengths and maintain my connection to the universe."

Maintaining connections to universes was something Vern knew a bit about by this point. He nodded wisely and lifted his glass. "Far out."

"Because here's the thing, Vern." She wondered again at how easy he was to talk to. "I fall too easily. And that's why

Greg broke my heart, and why my yoga instructor broke my heart, and why my nephew's algebra teacher broke my heart, and that realtor guy, and that—" She cut herself off and twirled her finger in an *etc. etc.* spiral.

"Wow."

Mia put her hands flat on the bar and spoke with conviction. "And that's why I'm not seeing anyone. I'm supposed to be building up my defenses first. I'm in a tunnel right now. I'm hibernating. Sheila says my heart is my strength. But it can only take so much before it's kaput. And then I'll get cold and bitter and then my one strength is gone and then who am I?"

"A very sad woman."

"A super sad woman."

"So, you're just gonna, what? Never fall in love?"

"Not until my heart is whole."

"When'll that be?"

"Not until at least after the summer solstice."

"What if the man of your dreams shows up before then?"

"He won't."

"How do you know?"

"Sheila read my charts."

"What if Sheila is full of it?"

"She's not."

"How do you know?

"I just do. I'm intuitive about people."

"Intuitive about yoga instructors and algebra teachers?"

Mia's expression contorted into a too familiar frown. "You're kind of an asshole."

"I'm just playing with you. I'm sorry. But I'm also glad."

"How come?"

"Cuz if you're telling me this, it means you're afraid you might fall for ME. Which means you like me."

"Oh is that so?"

"At least that's what my wiser voice tells me, deep down inside."

Mia snatched up her rag and twisted it and yanked it.

"Shut UP, Vern! How do you...?"

"How do I...?"

Vern realized what he had said, what his subconscious had accessed. The conversation that had tied him and Mia inexorably together back in his home universe, back on that glorious first night. Mia's divergent personality. Her smarter, wiser voice. His sense that she had been dancing just for him.

"Damn you, Vern," she muttered as she fixed him another drink.

Mia again returned to obsessively polishing a single spot on the bar. Vern wisely remained silent. A few decades passed. Mia stopped polishing.

"Okay, you can buy me a grouper sandwich."

"Great."

"But only as friends. No funny business."

"Deal. What time do you get done tonight?"

"Man, you don't dick around."

"Or tomorrow."

"Tomorrow I have a thing."

"A thing?"

"A garden party. At Sheila's."

"You don't want a grouper sandwich?"

"There will always be grouper sandwiches. Sheila only does this once a year. Her annual garden party. So how about this? You be my plus one. You'll love it, trust me."

"Sheila's, huh? What is it, this party? You gonna be, like, dancing around cauldrons or something?"

"No, shithead. It's a garden party. BBQ, nosh, probably a keg. It's a hoot."

"Right on. I'll bring all my crystals."

"Yeah?"

"Oh, yeah. I'm there."

"Just as friends, understand."

"Of course."

"Sheila would never approve otherwise."

"Yeah, yeah. I'll be your chaperone. Keep other lowbrows off your back. How's that work?"

"That works. And if you're a good boy, then you can buy me a grouper sandwich."

"Fuckin' excellent," said Vern.

And it was.

37

PAT LUEKE CROAKS

I t's quite tempting to treat your universe as the only one, isn't it?

Back in Vern's original sandbox, the campaign for Governor of Florida was still a-humming. Just a quick aside...

Pat Lueke had outperformed the Sneeds' most optimistic projections. Turns out there's a subset of voters who think unhinged, narcissistic bullies are the shit. The Sneeds had always flirted with this portion of the electorate but never dared to tap the source directly. Now they'd caught the tiger by the tail. Any ensuing chaos Lueke might cause as leader of the free world would be gravy. Already Lueke was sucking up so much oxygen that the Pontus Supreme explosion was entirely forgotten, and their bevy of under-the-table projects, safe from prying eyes now that all eyes were aghastedly affixed to their nominee, were free to accelerate and accumulate at intoxicating speed.

One detail about Pat Lueke that had yet to reach the newsrooms? He loved to read Rassmussen while on the toilet. Even with all his bravado, he—like the Sneeds—never thought he'd be doing quite this well. It was early in the campaign, granted.

But even in the nascent stages, his charm offensive was running roughshod. Lueke thought maybe the nostalgia factor was at play, but he was blissfully unaware that every blunt, spittle-soaked thing that fell from his mouth was being instantly added to a very clever series of internet memes curated by a well-funded "grassroots organization" that gave voice and vocabulary to that same portion of the population the Sneeds had learned to freebase.

Lueke scrolled on his phone and engaged his abdominals. He saw another baffled, breathless headline. He chuckled. He was the Pied Piper and his flute was rage. Millions of aimlessly angry people found so much endearing in witnessing him, a permanent fixture in "the establishment," reach his twilight and suddenly decide to tell "the truth." The fact that this alleged truth was 55 percent propaganda and 45 percent batshit anecdotes, non-sequiturs, tenuous metaphors, and oddly placed sound effects did not seem to deter a following that spanned nearly every demographic in all but thirteen states.

After his morning grunting, Lueke fried some bacon. Then he cooked three eggs in the bacon grease. Then he ate his satu-rated breakfast. Then he watched Sportscenter. Then he called his sister and emotionally assaulted her. Then he got dressed, called for the car, and died.

38

THE GARDEN PARTY

On his way home from work Vern stopped in at the St. Vincent De Paul Thrift Shop and acquired a second-hand Tommy Bahama camp shirt. People of Vern's sensibility often thought that brightly patterned linen shirts would help them assimilate into hip society. He took a bus to the edges of Indian Shores where he and Mia had agreed to meet at a 7-11. He popped in for a tin of Altoids and a six of Dos Equis and waited. After a meandering exchange with an old man dressed as a pirate who insisted that he'd run out of gas on his way to Tampa, Vern was relieved to see Mia emerging from the next bus, looking stunning and airy, carrying a covered casserole dish and a bottle of Gordon's gin.

"Been waiting long?" she asked.

"You have no idea."

They walked down a street lined with banyans and made a sharp turn down a gravel path marked only by a row of brightly colored mailboxes. They passed a row of run-down cracker homes, seemingly painted to match the mailboxes. Vern tried to place what sort of improvements had been made to this tract in the Queen Palm universe and determined that these twee, crumbling structures had likely been replaced. At the end of the lane, he and Mia approached a ramshackle but mystically charming bungalow. Vern pulled open the screen door for Mia.

The interior of the house was completely un-updated save for a few modern appliances. The furniture was thrown together and lacked any sort of stylistic unity, likely purchased at the Salvation Army or salvaged from curbs. Yet all of the dissonance conspired to create a fantastic level of social comfort. Crystals and salt lamps occupied every surface that wasn't otherwise crowded with the dips and drams, the at least nine different varieties of guacamole, and the countless crudité plates.

Representatives from every sect of the counter-culture populated the living room, their outfits and hairstyles reflecting their ages like strata in a canyon. Beatniks, hippies, punks, goths. Even a few bikers and a couple of ironic flappers. All engaged in intense conversations that could not be heard over the Eric Dolphy album playing on a miraculously functioning Victrola.

An animated, middle-aged woman in harem pants and a Wilco t-shirt emerged from a huddle sharing a hookah, and made a beeline for Mia and Vern.

"Mia! You made it!"

"Wouldn't miss it. Here. Artichoke dip." Mia placed the casserole dish on the last remaining empty spot on a side table. "And this is Vern. Vern, Sheila."

"How do, Vern?"

"Hi, thanks for having me."

"But of course!"

They shook hands. Sheila went "oooooh" then grabbed both of his hands and stared him down like a detective.

"Well. This is new," said Sheila.

"Yeah?" said Mia.

"What?" said Vern.

Sheila purred. "Hmmmmm. Very wild. The color he's giving off is kind of wispy. Kind of translucent."

"What's that mean?" Mia asked, hyper-curious, and Vern realized that he was being test-driven. Sneaky, sneaky Mia.

"I don't know. I've never seen it before." Sheila began to interrogate Vern. "You. Have you been to Japan in the past six months?"

"No."

"Recently ingested anything grown on a southern slope?"

"Um, I have no idea."

"Spoken with a long-lost relative?"

Vern wasn't sure if his mother would count in this circumstance. So he just shrugged and said, "Not sure."

Sheila gasped. "And it's breathing!"

"What's breathing?" asked Vern and Mia in unison.

"His color. Your color! Colors, really. They're expanding and contracting. Very hot. It's very, very, VERY hot." She turned to Mia. "Touch him. Touch his hand. Hold his hands."

Mia and Vern reached for each others' hands. Just when they were about to touch, Sheila shouted, "Stop! Freeze!"

Vern and Mia froze, hands in space, fingers extended toward each other. Sheila squatted and examined the space between them. She leaned in and sniffed the sliver of air between their digits. She sneezed, slowly stood, and swung her thickening gaze to Vern.

"Who the fuck are you?" she whispered.

Vern felt his mouth go dry. "Vern. Vern Cutler."

"Liar. Who are you and where did you come from?"

He tried on a charming smirk. "Funny you should ask." Sheila was not charmed.

Vern glanced at Mia, hoping she might bail him out, but

Mia was looking at him with a combination of fascination and suspicion.

Sheila gasped again.

"You have no tail!"

"Well that's a relief," said Vern.

"No, that's bad."

"Why is that bad?" Mia asked.

"Because it means he has no past." Sheila turned back to Vern. "You have no past." Sheila's gaze wavered between fear and pity.

He forced a laugh. "All we have is the present, right? Carpe diem and such?"

"Are you a cosmic blip or a spiritual vandal?" she asked him. Without waiting for an answer she turned again to Mia. "Mia, is he a cosmic blip or a spiritual vandal?"

"I'm sorry, Sheila," said Mia, " but I don't know what that means." Just then someone called to Sheila from across the room.

"Hey, Sheila! We're gonna make a run."

"Hang on!" she called back.

She took one more look at Vern and said "To be continued." She squeezed Mia's arm and disappeared into the crowd.

Vern and Mia stood close together, an eddy in the people streaming around them.

"She's a lot," said Mia.

"She's a character alright. Did I pass?"

"Don't know yet. And hey. Sorry about your tail."

They shared a deep and sincere laugh, their first in years, no bar between them, no weight of obligation pressing them down. Just two people genuinely attracted to each other, tail or no.

"You wanna see the garden?"

"Sure."

Mia put her bottle of gin on a classroom table that already sagged under the weight of a whole bevy of liquors and mixers. Vern unloaded his beer into an overflowing cooler. Mia mixed them a couple of gimlets—"the best cocktail for humid days"— and led him to the rear of the house.

When Vern stepped out onto the structurally compromised back porch of Sheila's bungalow he encountered what, in Queen Palm, would be a fever dream. There was a garden, yes. A sizable back yard contained by punk trees and bent bamboo and wisteria, but beyond this, in the northwest corner of the property, there was a direct inlet to the Gulf. His old instincts kicked in and his adrenals dumped buckets of *gimme-gimme* juice into his bloodstream. This was a two-million-dollar chunk of land he was standing on and here it was occupied by the shambly dwelling of a likely welfare recipient.

Mia felt him vibrating and ever so lightly patted him on his lower back. Her touch immediately depressurized his shoulders and distilled his robber baron proclivities into fast-dispersing vapors and inert aerosols. Some drifted harmlessly toward Cuba and some coasted, with no sense of purpose whatsoever, toward the Yucatan peninsula.

Vern caught his breath. No wonder people came down here for a quick visit and impulsively stayed for good. God, this must be how his Michigander parents felt when they first laid eyes on this particular green water, smelled this particular salt air, felt this particular wrapping-up heat. Why would you want to live anywhere else than here with that holy subtropical trinity of sand, surf, and sky bleeding and blending into each other?

With the proverbial scales fallen from his eyes, Vern took in the human activity in this unlikely utopia: a string band playing "Ripple" under a Spanish oak, a crude grill made from discarded cinder blocks holding a delicious array of slowly roasting kabobs and corn on the cob, a quartet of old ladies in a heated game of Spades at a picnic table, a young dude pushing his young swain on a tire swing. Revelers of every ilk eating, drinking, and making merry amid a late afternoon that seemed pre-fabricated especially for garden parties.

The Gulf welcomes all.

Vern and Mia spent the remaining daylight matching each other gimlet for gimlet. Mia introduced Vern to everyone she knew, each introduction more interesting than the last: a dread-locked philosophy professor, a raggae bassist, a Unitarian minister, a family of trapeze artists, and a whole assemblage of folks who'd found Sawnichickee to be the perfect place to be aimless and blissful, but who still managed to be intense and fascinating. One of them, a retired day trader in cut-off jean shorts, assisted Vern in performing his first keg stand since high school.

The sun began to set, as it does, as it must. Vern sat sprawled on a ratty tapestry and watched Mia wade into the Gulf, hiking her skirt up just shy of her shapely khyber. She stood in glorious physical abandon, half-devoured by the hypnotic waves, and sang to the setting sun as coastal windmills spun dutifully in the distance.

To Vern, there was no logic to any of it. It all seemed like one of those elective summer camps. Impractical whims were regarded with enough favor that they moved from impulsive conception to actual practice. And grown women got giddy at dusk. And there seemed to be no worry that some gears spun in a vacuum because it seemed that the machine was rapidly expanding and would soon interlock every component with some transcendent purpose. And despite all the incongruity, the only thing on Vern's mind was that maybe the man with all the tattoos would let him play his bongo drum for a while.

And once everyone had applauded the sun setting—no green flash tonight, but they'd watch for it again tomorrow—

that's exactly what the man with all the tattoos did. He gladly let Vern play his bongo drum.

Now, this may shock you, but Vern had always possessed an innate sense of rhythm. Tonight this natural aptitude manifested in a manner that could only be described as *bestial*. All the confusion and profound betrayal and hindsight and foresight and lust came roaring out like a ravenous daemon. The crunchy beach kids and lubricated party-goers immediately took a shine to Vern's raw, pulsing rhythms, and anything that could be co-opted as a percussion instrument was pressed into service. An impromptu circle formed. Vern felt tied to the universe. The drum was his heart. The drum was his blood. The air cooled a few degrees as his skin threatened to blister and the cleansing sweat poured, soaking his Tommy Bahama shirt till it dripped from the hem.

The ancient music swelled. Vern rode the brainwave of the cosmos and reached a level of elation beyond thought, beyond drooling, beyond sense of self, and at the height, at the HEIGHT... there was Mia. Standing by a tiki torch. Watching him. Adoring him.

He waited for an appropriate exit ramp in the beat and excused himself from the circle. No one noticed. They were all of one mind, and he had served his purpose as the tinder of the blaze.

In very few instances in any dimension could Vern be described as graceful. But the grace with which he returned those bongos to their owner and then glided toward Mia was pure Nureyev. He cradled her, she held on to him, he inhaled her musk, she pressed her palm to his forehead and his cheek. The sweat sizzled between them. The tiki flame samba'd in their eyes. And without speaking they agreed to wait on their imminent first kiss, not out of any sense of propriety or even fear of reprisal from Sheila, but because now that they both knew how the night would end, with lips and breath coming together, it was even more delicious to anticipate.

A light flashed and a whizz popped.

"C'mon," Mia said with a flick of her head.

They walked hand in hand past the drum circle to the patch of beach. On that moon-drenched white sand, a shirtless man with Seminole blood had begun a fiery light show employing Roman candles and Otis Redding. Because of course he had.

39

TABULA RASA

As the final fireworks and final notes of "Try a Little Tenderness" faded away, Vern noticed a light emerging from the cracked door of an old wooden tool shed. It beckoned. And on such a night and in such a place there is nothing to do but answer such a summons. Vern moved toward the door and slowly opened it.

Inside, an array of floodlights illuminated an in-progress painting on a large canvas. Standing in front of the canvas was an olive-skinned college kid gripping a pair of paintbrushes like nunchucks. His carpenter pants, splattered as they were with every color of paint in the painting, seemed to be an extension of it.

"Hey, man," said the painter, "come on in."

Vern stepped into the glow of the shed and took in the images. On the left half of the canvas was a trippy, Van Gogh-y color field embossed with the image of a baby in utero. The painter had somehow balanced abstraction with hyper-realism. The baby was as fragile and papery as one might expect but the painter had defied obstetric convention by allowing the unborn child's eyelids to part, revealing the piercing orbs beneath. On the right half of the canvas, in an unassuming stenciled font, were the words "Tabula Rasa."

Vern was instantly transported back to the plane of existence he had traveled while drumming. He didn't have the vocabulary to describe what this painting was doing to him in critical terms. All he could muster in the moment was, "Hey. That's just... That's real good."

"Thanks, man."

"What's that mean? Tab-yoo-lah raise-uh?"

"Tabula rasa," said the painter. "Blank slate, man."

"Blank slate?"

"Blank slate."

Vern's mind whirled. He and the painter stared at the painting in silence. The painter went "*mmrrrrr*," sorta like the growl of a dreaming dog. The painter made one tiny adjustment with one of his brushes. Vern couldn't see what had changed, but the painter huffed contentedly, and Vern felt the painting somehow throb. Vern's words again failed him utterly.

"Like... the baby. It's a blank slate."

"Yeah, man."

"Like, no harms. No fouls. No—"

"Preconceptions. No prejudice. No cynicism."

"No sins. No cares. No regrets. Nice, clean, pink lungs."

"A totally fresh canvas, man. Like this canvas used to be. Fresh canvas on top of fresh canvas."

Vern considered the implications and tried to imagine what it must feel like to be that pristine and unencumbered, with a vast expanse of virginal possibility before oneself. And then he realized he was feeling that way right now. That he had been feeling exactly that since taking the job at Johnny's. That he himself was canvas on canvas, and how sad it was that no one can remember how that feels, how we all of us forget it, are forced to forget it, and how complicit we all are in dashing and daunting and dismantling it. And why was he the lucky one to see and understand? To feel what everyone by simple right of being human ought to be allowed to feel? His diaphragm spasmed. His eyes watered. He choked on on a gasp of hot, dusty, paint-stained air.

"You alright, man?"

Vern fought his tears, unsuccessfully. He began to mewl.

Mia poked her head in the door. "Are you guys toking without me?"

The painter looked at her and then at Vern who had progressed to weeping openly. There was no judgment or discomfort in the painter's eyes. Only mild concern.

"Vern?" said Mia. "Vern, you okay?"

Vern motioned toward the painting.

"*Look* at it," he said. And then he cried some more.

"Vern... Oh, honey."

He gestured again to the canvas.

"It's just... so... *true.*"

Mia again gently patted his lower back. He collapsed against her, then turned and hugged her hard. She was taken aback at first. Then she caressed his shoulder blades. His rib cage expanded and contracted with the throes of his tears.

"Sweet Jesus," he mumbled into her hair. "I'm so sorry, Mia."

"Sorry for what? Everything's okay."

He held her for a beat longer, then released her from his embrace and regained, oh, say sixty-two percent of his composure.

"Forgive me," he said to the painter. "Your painting... that caught me off guard." He shook it off, rubbed his face, tousled his hair. "Whew! You know?"

"Hell yeah," said the painter. "You want it?"

"Do I...?"

The painter nodded.

"I don't have any money on me."

Mia took a step toward the door. "My purse is in the house, I'll—"

"That's okay." said the painter, waving her off. "He should have it. No worries. You should have it, man"

"But... Really?"

"Yeah really."

Vern hugged the painter tighter than he'd ever hugged a grown man. The painter hugged him back.

"Thank you," Vern whispered.

"It's alright, Brother. I got you."

Later, Vern and Mia walked back down the gravel path. The Tabula Rasa was wrapped in brown paper and tucked safely under Vern's arm. The moon illuminated their way, the cicadas composed impromptu tone poems, the breeze whispered conspiratorially with the palm trees. Mia stopped abruptly.

"You okay, Mia?"

She didn't say anything for a beat, then mustered, "Thanks for coming with me."

"Are you kidding? Thanks for inviting me. It was a blast."

"I gotta say... I'm awful fond of that soul of yours."

"Yeah?" said Vern. "I hardly knew I had one."

"Well, you do."

"Nah."

"And it's a sweet one. I mean it."

"Just the tip of a big ugly iceberg."

"Vern."

"OK. OK. Thank you. Your soul is sweet, too."

Their anticipation, held in check for about as long as humanely possible, scrabbled and strained. The cicadas fortissimo'd. So much so that Vern heard Mia's breathy "Kiss me?" more with the hairs on his arms than with his ears.

It felt like hours before they unyoked. When they did, they both knew they would feel the aftershocks of that kiss until their respective far-off future passings. They stood together tightly, his chin upon her head, her cheek against his chest. They breathed. And things made so much damn sense.

"Did you just come out of your tunnel?" asked Vern.

"I think I did," said Mia.

40

WHAT DREAMS MAY COME

M ia had been renting the top floor of a carriage house situated among banyan trees behind a stately home that had been built by one of Sawnichickee's first Yankee settlers and was now lovingly maintained and resided in by a married pair of marine biologists. Both structures were built of cypress and compressed coquina shells, and were designed in such a way that, in the days before air conditioning, the breezes from the Gulf were free to circulate unimpeded. What resulted was a series of salty wind tunnels that simultaneously cooled the inhabitants, dispersed the dense oppression of the region's infamous humidity, and even delivered the occasional aroma of magnolia and orange blossom.

Vern and Mia walked, hand in hand, Mia leading, neither speaking, both saying everything. They rounded the corner of Gumpertz Lane and the main house came into view.

"This is me," she said.

"Jesus!" said Vern.

"I know, it's gorgeous, but I'm just the carriage house in back."

"No, I mean this is like four blocks from where I grew up."

"You're kidding!"

"No, yeah, right over..." He pointed off into the night.

"How about that."

They smiled at each other. Both wondered if she would or should invite him in. Their fleshes and spirits were willing, no doubt, but both still floated on the vapors of that kiss, and both realized they were loathe to cheapen an evening that had been, to this point, an anagogic rapture.

"I'm all in here," Vern said.

"Me too," Mia said.

"No hurry."

"No rush."

She stretched up on her tiptoes and brushed her lips with exquisitely torturous precision on the corner of his mouth. His breath audibly caught. She smirked gleefully to herself, enjoying on a molecular level how her effect on him affected her. She walked along the side of the house, leaving Vern dizzy on the sidewalk. She climbed the carriage house steps. Just before opening the door, she looked back. Vern had moved a few steps to the side, so he could look past the main house and see her moonlit silhouette up there all like Juliet on her balcony.

Not wanting to wake the marine biologists, she stage whispered, "You still owe me a grouper sandwich," and disappeared inside.

Vern's elation hit a palpable crescendo. Mia, he loved. Grouper sandwiches, likewise. But the promise of both in combination provoked such a surge in serotonin production that Vern knew he'd never get to sleep that night.

Except he did. After floating home to his motel room—which he'd be moving out of next week, thank you very much! —and dancing with every lamppost along the way, he took a quick rinse in the shower and fell into his bed giggling, and was asleep before he could even turn off the bedside light.

His last conscious thought was, "Now I can dream of her."

But, as much as we'd like them to, our subconscious lives are frustratingly reluctant to pander to their target audience. As much as we'd like our slumber to be an extension of whatever pleasure our waking lives have mustered, our dreams are too often dead set on neglecting our fancies. And so Vern, rather than dreaming of Mia at sunset, was carried by Morpheus back to Queen Palm...

The oil spill had reached local shores, rendering the waters black as tar. Sea turtles were dragging themselves out of the Gulf, collecting their eggs, and boarding FEMA planes. The sun was masked by a translucent haze of gray and Vern was standing naked in front of a horde of torch-wielding retirees. Vern bolted, they pursued. Meteors occasionally collided with the earth in front of him. Vern came to an open field littered with steaming piles of excrement which he, barefoot, endeavored to avoid but couldn't.

When he reached the edge of the shit field, Vern was relieved to find himself at the dog track. He rushed inside hoping to evade the angry geriatrics who were still, astonishingly, on his tail. Despite his lack of pockets he produced a twenty-dollar bill and approached the window where he placed a boxed trifecta bet on three greyhounds named 'Nads Golden, Certain Doom, and Debbie Harry. The cashier, a dead ringer for Paul Lynde, rolled his eyes dismissively and muttered, "Good luck."

Vern bought a beer that disappeared from his hands and made his way to the track. The race was already in progress. Debbie Harry was leading the pack with Certain Doom and 'Nads Golden close behind. But another dog, a Siberian Husky named Fickle Finger, was quickly gaining. Vern was about to file a complaint about Fickle's unacceptable pedigree when 'Nads Golden suddenly mounted Debbie Harry from behind, allowing the other dogs to pass. Certain Doom won by a yard but this was a pyrrhic victory for Vern given his other two picks, distracted by making puppies, had yet to cross the finish line. And wouldn't you know it, the AARP mob, torches aloft, had reached the snack bar.

Frantically seeking an escape route Vern scaled the chain-link fence surrounding the track. The fence held back the horde but now the dogs took up the chase. Vern ran around the oval. The mechanical rabbit remained just out of reach and taunted him by singing Jimmy Buffet in a minor key. WWI fighter jets shaped like pelicans flew overhead, divebombing and strafing. And then Vern saw at the far end of the track the earth opening. A chasm formed, swallowing the scoreboard and a few greyhounds whose plaintive howls echoed. He skittered to a stop at the edge of the abyss. A finger tapped him on the shoulder. He turned and there stood D'Angelo, shaking his head sadly. Both of D'Angelo's arms were wrapped, wrist to bicep, with various wristwatches. He placed one hand on Vern's chest.

"Sorry, mate."

D'Angelo shoved. Vern lost his footing and toppled over the edge. He hurtled for hours through an endless slideshow of his failures and humiliations.

Vern awoke soaking wet and hyperventilating. He groped his way to the bathroom, slapped water on his face, and looked in the mirror. The Vern in the mirror looked back with conviction and said, "I'm never going back."

Vern should have known better. You don't say things into mirrors. Bloody Mary, Candyman, Beetlejuice? You want to conjure a boogeyman, say some goddamn nonsense into the mirror.

41

EVEN PLUTOCRATIC LIZARD PEOPLE GET THE BLUES

The Sneeds, though emotionless reptiles beneath their human disguises, were crestfallen to receive the news of Pat Lueke's demise. Their under-endowed limbic systems were incapable of developing any real fondness or warmth for him, but they felt the loss, all the same. Their grieving process began by blaming one another for not forcing Lueke to have a physical exam before throwing all that money at him. There they stood, the veritable puppeteers of Western humanity, near blows, every howling word punctuated with consonants that sent fine sprays of spittle into one another's eyes.

Both men knew, as would anyone, that the conversation was rather moot. Whoever did or didn't see to this or that before things were set in motion was an irrelevant consideration. But it allowed their synapses to continue firing while their pragmatic brains slowly awoke to the realization that their brotherly throwdown had nothing to do with Lueke and everything to do with the reality that they had no backup plan. Because even though Lueke was ancient and overweight and diabetic, even though, had he lived, he probably would've derailed his campaign with a glib comment anyway, and even though they never, in their wildest wettest dreams, had ever imagined that Lueke would do so well... they also had never taken the time to notice that, in the clear, remorseless light of day, they had not one other viable candidate in their stable.

When all the recriminations and spitting were over, the Sneed brothers stood silently in front of their cold fireplace for nearly four solid minutes. Then they began to consider their options. Malcolm paced. Sandy crossed to the window and looked out at the gators sunning themselves.

"Is Swallerman entirely out of the question?" asked Malcolm.

"The daughter's now making six figures a month on something called OnlyFans. She wields a riding crop. It won't do."

"Dunne?"

"Another starlet fling."

"Pringle?"

"Grand jury."

Malcolm dramatically shoved a stack of folders off his desk.

"Our only choice..." Sandy closed his eyes and girded his loins. "...appears to be Wesley Schla."

"The stutterer??" Malcolm had little patience for stutterers.

"We have him on an experimental Russian anxiety inhibitor. I haven't heard yet whether it's working."

"Schla?"

"Yes."

"SCHLA??"

"YES."

"Out of the goddamn question!" Malcolm dramatically threw a fountain pen across the room.

Sandy turned and hissed at his brother. "Then we offer no candidate."

Malcolm pouted and kicked at the carpet with his Bostonians. He knew there was no way they could sit out even a blessed millisecond of an election cycle. It wasn't even about winning. They just needed a voice to yank the party toward their preferred platform, which more and more meant heaping piles of raw red meat in front of the most voracious pack of primary voters. But Schla?? They had to maintain *some* standards.

The brothers sat at their twin desks, deflated and defeated.

Sandy glanced up at the wall full of monitors. Pringle's indictment had just come through that morning. All the news channels were breathlessly replaying the footage of her standing on the courthouse stairs next to her blustering lawyer. Sandy saw her face at this angle, that angle, good side, bad side, eye level, from below. So many Pringles.

So many Pringles.

An idea leaped fully formed into Sandy's consciousness. He knew Malcolm would resist, so he counted to ten before speaking, giving himself time to choose the best way to massage his brother.

Sandy sighed loudly. Malcolm looked over.

"What?"

"Oh. I was just thinking," Sandy said. "It's a shame about Bushnell. The amount of time we put into that kid."

"And the money," growled Malcolm.

"Sure."

Sandy counted to ten again, hoping the hook was set. He yanked.

"But you know... maybe we could bring him back."

Malcolm snorted. "Bring him back?"

"Yes."

"Bushnell?!"

"Yes."

"Out of the goddamn question!" Malcolm dramatically heaved a pad of post-it notes into the fireplace.

"Listen, he lost his composure. Maybe we weren't supporting him as we should've been. Maybe we were taking him for granted. You know how sentimental—"

"You're out of your mind."

"Everyone's all but forgotten about the damned oil spill."

"There's a federal investigation!"

Sandy held up a professorial finger. "A simple 'I'm sorry' goes a long way with these types of people. Then we set him up, see? All the worries that made him come unglued, we take care of. He's a fine-looking man and he talks such a good game. Really, Malcolm. We just have to make him feel special again."

Sandy watched Malcolm work it through.

"But we removed him from the universe."

Sandy shrugged like such things happened every day. "Temporarily."

"How do we explain that?"

"We just tell him, you know, that we were looking out for his best interests."

"No, Sandy. To the public. How do we explain that to the *public*? A Congressman and candidate for Governor disappears for weeks and then just pops back in like nothing happened?"

Sandy smiled.

"We say he was hiking the Appalachian Trail."

42

SHEILA MAKES THE BLOCK HOT

Sheila had watched Mia's moth circling Vern's flame the entire night at the party. She had watched them leave together. So the next morning, as Vern was talking to himself in the mirror and the Sneed Brothers were plotting in their lair (though how the whole notion of "simultaneously" works across universes is something you don't want to spend too much time thinking about; guaranteed migraine), Sheila rang up her acolyte.

"Have a nice time last night?"

"Sheila you have no idea!"

"Except I do. I think you should come in this afternoon."

Now, there were a number of things Sheila believed deeply. Enough so to divvy them up into three categories. First, there were those beliefs which, though skeptics might look at them askance, were basically mainstream. She shared these beliefs with a significant portion of the population and made herself a comfy living trading in them. She believed in the healing power of crystals. She believed that Tarot cards were siphons for inner wisdom and spiritual self-knowledge. She believed charting the placement of the stars and planets at the time of one's birth could give one a fairly firm handle on their life's trajectory. Although there was little in the way of empirical evidence to confirm these beliefs, any truly open-minded person would do well not to cast self-righteous aspersions on them. Certainly you, privy now as you are to the existence of parallel universes and the mind-blowing workings of the Project, know that these notions hold, at the very least, a thimble-full of water.

Next, there were a handful of things Sheila believed that were of questionable veracity at best. She believed, for example, that sauerkraut cured cancer and that she could communicate cogently with dolphins. While not overtly harmful, these beliefs were enough on the fringe that even Sheila knew to hold back from sharing them except with those she knew in advance were likely to sympathize if not outright agree. In these examples, while a truly open-minded person would not claim to know with absolute certainty that Sheila was wrong—absolutely certainty and open-mindedness are sworn enemies, after all—they could also reasonably suspect that she might be half-crocked.

This brings us to the final category, which is those beliefs that Sheila clung to in defiance of the most minimal objective observation. Prime example: she believed that sandalwood effectively masked the smell of cat piss. This was easily refuted by spending any amount of time in her salon. She also believed that a cabal of politicians, Hollywood elites, professional athletes, and hospital executives was in the process of bending the entire population of the Earth to their will and had achieved immortality by drinking smoothies made from stem cells harvested from the placentas of newborn babies. This was not only easily disproven by a rudimentary understanding of hematology but was also a living illustration of the Venn diagram shared by some New Age devotees and most fascists.

Sheila hadn't laid any Category Three wisdom on Mia yet, which explained Mia's obeisance to most of Sheila's less sinister notions.

But Mia was struggling mightily this afternoon, not only with the logistics of breathing through her mouth whenever the aroma of cat urine threatened to overwhelm her olfactory equilibrium but most especially with Sheila's clamorous insistence that Vern had no tail.

"What does that even mean??"

"It means he's transient, Mia! It means he's cosmically unglued. It wouldn't worry me so much if you weren't so susceptible."

There was that word again. "Susceptible." Sheila had diagnosed Mia as "susceptible" on their first meeting. And every time Mia thought she'd crawled out of a hole or made a breakthrough, Sheila was always there to remind her just how thin her skin was, how jaundiced her aura, and how vital it was that she maintain a degree of caution.

"But you didn't see him with that painting, Sheila. He's sensitive, he's patient, he's..." Mia stopped herself from saying "able to make my toes curl with his kiss." Such a detail wasn't likely to help her cause.

"Listen, Mia, sociopaths seem sensitive and patient. There are some souls which are so odious that no temporality can accommodate them. So they move through their lives taking meals where they can and leaving spiritual bones and crumbs behind, where once there was bounty. Sometimes it's for the sake of survival and other times it's just pure malevolence."

"Vern's not odious! Or malevolent!"

"But he's certainly hungry."

"Isn't everyone? If I'm in a tunnel, what am *I* supposed to eat?"

"But you only have the psychic sustenance to maintain your own survival. There's not enough of you to feed him too!"

Mia had run out of viable metaphors with which to defend herself. Sheila was relentless.

"I can't believe you're even considering coming out of your tunnel. After all the progress we've made. You're healing, Mia. You are. But all you have to do is look at your chart and you'll see how devastating it would be to jump the gun on this. Last night happened, it's over, fine, nothing to be done, but there's no reason to throw good money after bad."

"It's just grouper sandwiches!"

Sheila laid a card on the table and gasped.

"Oh shit."

"What?"

"A reversed Ten of Cups..."

"And?"

"Disconnection... misaligned values... broken relationships... Mia, honey, you haven't even had your first real date with this man and you're already right back where you started." Sheila clucked her tongue, re-shuffled the cards. "What a shame."

Usually, when Sheila clucked, Mia crumbled. But not this time. Something was different. Being out of her tunnel didn't feel scary... it felt so damn *goooood*. Sure, part of that was Vern. Oh Vern. Vern with his patterned shirts and the imperfect poetry of his tongue and the fact that, at his age, he was working at a car wash. But wasn't she working at a bar? And didn't she love working at that bar? She had listened with fascination more than once while serving Vern bourbon as he waxed poetic about the finer points of waxing and detailing. Expertise in anything was sexy as hell.

Mia realized this feeling of lung expanded strength and freedom was not only because of Vern. It was because of her, too. Her own work. If Sheila truly believed what she claimed to believe, why couldn't it be that Vern had only manifested because Mia conjured him? Because Mia was ready? So what if he didn't have a tail? Wasn't taillessness in itself a state of "susceptibility"?

Mia left the furiously clucking Sheila. She worked her shift at the Azure Tides in a blissful cloud of anticipation. She blushed head to toe when Vern called her work phone from his work phone on his break. She pictured him massaging a front panel, covered in sudsy lather. They made their plans.

Mia hung up more certain of Vern than she'd been of anything in decades. You might even say she felt absolute certainty.

43

CAPTAIN GORDO'S GROUPER
SANDWICH RECIPE

"Lard. You gotta use lard. If you want to mix in a little Canola oil, just to be health-conscious, I suppose you can. But get that lard good and hot. Now you got two bowls. In one of 'em you got your flour and your cornmeal and some white pepper and some black pepper and some onion salt and a little paprika. Sometimes I do a little cayenne, not today. In the other bowl a bottle of Miller Genuine Draft, an egg, a few drops of Crystal hot sauce... whisk it up. Then you take your grouper, see? And dip her in the beer and egg, dredge her in the flour, dip her in the egg again, dredge her some more. Sometimes I have to do this three times depending on the disposition of the fish, but you want a nice coating. Then put her in the hot lard, 'bout 350 degrees, and let her cook in there for, oh, six minutes or so. Lay her out on a paper towel for a minute and hit her with a little salt. Get a bun... I like a good potato roll but some folks think that's sacrilegious... tartar sauce, we make our own, that's the wife's department. And that's about it. How you like 'em?"

"The best," said Mia around a huge bite. "The absolute best."

Vern agreed with a nod, his mouth too full to do anything but grunt. He held up his empty beer bottle.

"Well, lookie there." Captain Gordo let out a resonant belly laugh, "You're drinking on credit, ain't you? Hang tight. I'll grab you another beer. You folks enjoy."

Captain Gordo's did not exist in Queen Palm anymore. After thirty years in business, it had been replaced by a Walgreen's. Vern hadn't had the pleasure of one of Captain Gordo's grouper sandwiches in years and had never imagined he'd ever have one again. This was just one more benefit of astral projection. The biggest benefit was sitting across the table from him, devouring her sandwich with a seductive dearth of tact. Vern derived great pleasure from observing her enjoyment. He was also fairly grooving on the unusually mild day, his creeping beer buzz, the budding sunset.

Mia finished the last precious bite and looked at Vern with an expression of supreme satisfaction. She even burped, with no apology, her chest rumbling with contentment. Vern snickered.

"Oh like you don't," Mia teased.

Vern took a quick swig, worked the froth in his throat, answered Mia with an airy belch. They laughed, oblivious to anything and anyone but each other.

Later, having walked to the waterside public park looking out over the bay—another piece of paved paradise back in Queen Palm, Vern noted—they sat side-by-side on a suspended bench swing and watched the sun play hide and seek in the color-shifting clouds. His hand rested lightly on her thigh like it had been carved to fit. Her fingers played lightly on the nape of his neck, idly twirling his hair.

There was nowhere else either of them would rather be.

"Hey, Vern?"

"Hmm?"

"Where were you?"

"Huh?"

"When you went away, left Sawnichickee. Where'd you go?"

It had never occurred to Vern to prepare an answer for this most obvious of questions.

"You know. Here and there."

"Mmm. Population everyone."

She smiled. He smiled back. Hers was warm and without judgment. His was nervous. She could tell.

"Vern, I had a session with Sheila yesterday."

"Good ol' Sheila."

"She told me I oughta stay away from you."

"She didn't like my drumming?"

Mia giggled and took his hand in both of hers.

"Listen, it doesn't matter to me where you've been before you walked into my bar. What you did, who you hurt, how you hurt them, how they hurt you. You've got a blank slate with me, y'know? You only ever have to tell me what you think you need to tell me. But anything before you and me? Has nothing to do with me."

Vern couldn't believe what he was hearing. He felt tears welling, but dammit he couldn't cry in front of her already *again*, could he? He lifted her hands, kissed them, pressed them against his face.

"Thank you."

She smiled at him. Her smile cracked the heavens opened. The molten core of the earth throbbed. He saw the inner mathematical truths of time and space falling like pixie dust into the sea. He loved her. And he knew he could never lie to her, but how could he tell Mia the truth without her thinking he was mentally unbalanced?

Mia provided the answer. "Anyhow, Sheila went on and on about how you've got no tail and whatnot—"

"Oh I got a tail, baby."

"I don't care whether you do or don't, Vern. But Sheila wouldn't let up and she's really bent out of shape about me and my tunnel. Like, I know she cares, but geez. I'm a grown-ass woman, y'know?"

Vern could see that Mia meant what she said, but that she was also on foal-legs when it came to being out of her tunnel. Sheila's opinion still held powerful sway. In Queen Palm, Sheila could've been dealt with. Bought off. Blackmailed. Publicly smeared. But in Sawnichickee, not only did Vern lack the political infrastructure to carry out such plans, but he quite sincerely didn't want to do any of that. The underhanded strategery that had always been a fun bit of sport for him held no allure whatsoever. Sheila was a complete moonbat but if anyone in this universe was capable of believing Vern's unbelievable story, it was her. And if she was half as perceptive as she claimed to be, surely upon hearing the explanation for his tail-lessness she'd detect the undeniably star-crossed rapport twixt Vern and Mia. Sheila's blessing procured, he and Mia could be off to the races.

So, as a placeholder of sorts, Vern told Mia about a trip he'd taken to Los Angeles. It was not a robust answer to her question about where he'd been, it did not explain his thirty-year absence from Sawnichickee, but it was not a lie. Vern walked her home again. They shared several more blistering kisses on the sidewalk—Vern even caught the marine biologists peeking at them through a curtain—and it was clear what Mia intended, but Vern didn't want even the whiff of advantage being taken to soil their first time, so he extricated himself and while standing under the coldest of cold showers resolved to make his first appointment with a bonafide spiritual advisor. Post-friggin'-haste.

44

MARTIN BUBER'S PHILOSOPHY OF DIALOGUE

Chimes dinged secrets to each other as Vern opened the door to the New Age bookstore/herbalist/matcha stand/bicycle shop/subversive occultist enclave where Sheila worked part-time. She didn't look up from the counter where she was unpacking a box of apothecary bottles.

"Had a feeling you'd be stopping by today."

Vern attempted a joke. "Of course you did."

Sheila harrumphed.

"Can we talk, Sheila?"

"Sure we can. Whether we'll communicate? Well." Now she did look up and Vern could feel her eyes scanning him like a killer cyborg from the future. "Let me lock up here. I'll take an early lunch and we can speak privately in my salon."

"Great. Thank you."

"Thanks are premature. Wait outside."

Vern stepped back out onto the sidewalk at the perfect moment to witness a minor traffic accident that played out like a command performance just for him. A dignified older gentleman in a Lincoln Town Car had stopped abruptly to avoid slaughtering a squirrel. Then came a screech of tires and a sonorous thud from the impact of a Ford Fiesta's fender against the Town Car's bumper. A sun-burned woman in yoga pants sprang from the Fiesta and immediately gave the old man what-for. The squirrel perched on the side of the road a few feet down from Vern, watching its handiwork and munching a seed like popcorn. The woman's finger jabbed and jabbed in the old man's face. The old man kept wiping the sheen from his forehead with a monogrammed handkerchief. Vern wondered at the inevitable randomness—or was it the random inevitableness?—of collisions.

The door opened, startling Vern and the squirrel. The critter zipped away. Vern waited for Sheila to work the locks. She finished and gave him that assessing, X-ray look again.

"Let's go."

He followed her down the strip a couple of blocks and up the gravel path.

Ever been in a club or restaurant before opening, under work lights? Ambiance is a vampire; direct light murders it. But Sheila's bungalow on that little piece of Gulf shore... even in the indifferent light of mid-day, Vern felt the drum-heartbeat of the place. The tool shed where he'd met the painter still had an aura of magic about it. He paused for a moment. And just breathed.

"Come on then," Sheila lobbed at him from the porch.

"Here we go," Vern thought to himself.

Sheila admitted Vern into her salon. As she smudged the place with sage, Vern took a deep, thoughtful gander at Sheila's lair. It looked like some kind of haphazard pagan shrine, but, strangely, he felt no scorn. Even when he choked momentarily, first on the sage smoke and then on the cat piss, he couldn't bring himself to loathe any of the ideas behind any of the trinkets or wall hangings or carpets or vials.

"Some place," said Vern.

Sheila stubbed out the smudge stick in a wobbly brass bowl. "Please, sit down."

Vern lowered himself unsteadily onto a boho bean bag. A shriek coalesced into a violently sibilant hiss. A disgruntled Siamese cat darted from behind the bean bag, through the beaded curtains, and into the next room. Vern yelped, too— "*Jesus!*"—and leaped out of the bean bag. He felt some minor ligament pop.

"Martin Buber, actually."

"Huh?"

"The Austrian philosopher. I inherited him from my theology professor when he passed."

"The cat, you mean?"

"Yes. The cat."

"Well, I'm sorry I spooked... Martin Buber."

"No worries. He's very resilient. I have a chair if you prefer."

"It's fine." Vern lowered himself back onto the beanbag and massaged his calf.

Sheila sat across from him, took a huge, grounding breath, and zapped him with her look again. This time it felt like she was peeling back his skin, layer by layer. It occurred to Vern that the expression on her face was one of constipation, but he thought this without judgment. Whatever spiritualistic dressing-down ceremony she was preparing likely took a similar amount of concentration.

"I would normally ask a new client to focus deeply on an aspect of their life that needs guidance," Sheila said.

"But we both already know why I'm here."

"Yes. We do. Well, Vern. May I call you Vern? Vern. There are two issues. One. Mia is in no condition to take someone on. Naturally, she possesses free will and can conduct herself as she chooses but, in my function as her, you know, her—"

"Spiritual advisor?"

"Indeed. I can and will continue to advise her against engaging romantically with anyone until her heart is buttressed."

"And Issue Two, I'm guessing, is me in particular."

"Affirmative."

"Because of my tail."

"Your lack of one."

"Have you ever seen anyone else without a tail before?" Vern asked with sincere curiosity.

"Yes, but not like you."

"Really? What do you mean?"

Another cat wandered in and settled onto Sheila's lap as she considered her answer.

"I've run across a few people who lost their memories. Their tails aren't there, but the very absence of the tail is there. Like a phantom limb, or the negative of a photograph, or the way after you look directly at the sun then close your eyes you still see it on the inside of your lids?"

Vern nodded. "OK, yeah, sure."

"I've seen something similar in a few people who've had psychotic breaks, tails which are perceivable by the vacuum they've left behind. I've seen people possessed, but that results in two or more tails, not the absence of one."

Vern's mouth hung open. He was utterly fascinated. Another cat wandered in, settled in his lap. He scratched its ears without thinking.

"Then there are people suffering from PTS."

"Trauma?"

"Mmhmm. That can vary from tails that have been severed and writhe along behind people like a pet snake, to tails with missing segments, to tails that are wrapped around their throats."

"I mean... wow."

Another cat wandered in. Both of Sheila's hands idly ruffled fur. Martin Buber still stayed away.

"But you, Vern. You are a new one for me. Your tail quite simply does not exist. No shadow. No vacuum. No pieces. Nothing. To be fair you've got a nub."

"A *nub*?"

"Like you just were born just a few weeks ago, like you popped into existence with no history of your previous fifty-whatever years attached. This phenomenon I have never seen. And, to be perfectly frank, Vern, it freaks my shit out."

They sat silent for a moment, petting purring cats.

"Sheila, I want to let you in on something. This whole 'open-minded' thing is very new for me, okay?"

"Clearly."

"Now you say I have no tail. Let's say I concede the point."

"So you admit it?"

"I'm conceding the possibility as a way to set up a thought experiment."

Sheila narrowed her eyes. "OK."

"OK. So. Hypothetically, if I have no tail, what does that mean? Is a tail one hundred percent necessary? Can a person live without one?"

"You seem to be doing fine. But, hypothetically, it would be highly worrisome."

"Why?"

"Because there's nothing so desperate and dangerous as a spiritual fugitive."

This stung Vern. He'd been called a lot of things in his day: douchebag, sociopath, corporate stooge, lapdog to the oligarchy, fuggin' prick, carpet bagger, butt head, dick head,

shit head, boot licker, poon hound, congressional fluffer, igno-
rant hayseed, classless heel, and so on. But "spiritual fugitive"
put a painfully accurate name to a chronic condition. What
Sheila had intuited was more than Vern's current displace-
ment. It was a trend toward incorporeal itinerancy that had
been a part of Vern's constitution since he stood at that
payphone at the 7-11, Malcolm Sneed's business card in hand,
all those years ago.

Vern licked his wounded pride as the cat on his lap likewise
licked itself clean. Sheila looked on with no small amount of
satisfaction.

"So it's my fault I don't have a tail?" Vern asked quietly.

Sheila softened. "Yes and no."

"Okay, listen..." began Vern.

And then he filled this veritable stranger in on the whole
wild tale. Queen Palm and the other Mia and the Sneeds and
the Project. The Pontus Supreme explosion, his kidnapping,
the agent named D'Angelo, his waking up in a parallel
universe. He did not spare himself in the retelling. He spelled
out all his sins and trespasses along the way. He even told her
about the dream.

"And it still feels like I'm falling, Sheila."

Without speaking she got up and left the room. The
displaced cats oozed over and tucked into various crevices
along his body. Sheila returned with a glass of sparkling water.
She handed it to him. "So I guess... welcome to our universe."

"Thanks." He took the glass and drank gratefully.

Sheila sat back down and assessed him again, but now her
cyborg/x-ray/skin-flaying eyes were gentle, like a nurse sponge-
bathing away layers of dust and blood and grime.

"I believe you, Vern. All the goddesses help me, I believe
you. You know why?"

He shook his head, covered in cats.

"Because you didn't try to convince me of your redemption. You didn't make any excuses."

Vern finished the water.

"More?"

He shook his head, set the glass aside, re-filled his hands with felines.

Sheila chewed her lip. "So my bungalow is gone in your other universe?"

"Can't say for sure, but can't imagine it survived the developers."

"And are Mia and I friends?"

Vern shrugged. "No idea. I think I would remember if I'd met you back there, but I never really knew what Mia did with her days. It's conceivable you and she could have crossed paths, but if you did she never mentioned it to me. Do you still think I'm a spiritual fugitive?"

"Oh yes. But the thing about fugitives, Vern... they are all running away from something. And some somethings are worth running away from. The question for you now is... what are you running TO?"

Vern thought he'd never in his life heard something so damn wise.

Sheila smirked. "Confession. I got that from a fortune cookie. But it's apt, no?"

"Crazy apt."

A timer bonged. Sheila stood and shooed away the cats.

"Walk me back to work? Lunch is up."

"Of course. Thank you for hearing me out."

On the walk back, Sheila said, "So you really squandered your relationship with Mia back there, huh?"

"Big time."

"And you're not going back?"

"Hell no."

Sheila glanced at him. "I'm envious, in a way. What I wouldn't give to travel another universe..."

They arrived at the shop. The fender bender had been cleared. The squirrel was back out in the middle of the road.

Sheila got out her keys. "I can't give you my outright blessing. Not yet. But I'm much better at this open-minded thing than you are, so here's the deal. You might be what Mia needs. But you have to tell her everything, like you just told me."

"I was afraid you were going to say that."

"It's the only way, Vern."

"I know, Sheila."

"Be quick about it."

"I'm seeing her this evening. I'll tell her everything. You have my word."

45

VERN IS SUMMONED HOME

That evening, Vern arrived at the tiki bar early, hours before Mia was due to rendevous. He was beyond nervous. As the afternoon wore on and he tried out his story over and over again in his motel mirror, his excitement at procuring Sheila's blessing melted into puddles of fear. Should he just blurt it out? Should he try to ease in? Dare he talk about all the variations of tails? Or maybe dazzle her with impossible knowledge, stuff he could only know because another her had told him in another universe? Stuff like "Hey Mia, did you or did you not get your one and only spanking when you were eight and cut your own hair? And did you not break your arm sliding into third during the 1986 Florida State High School Softball finals?" Wait, shit, it was second base. "And were you or were you not obsessed with Dolly Parton for the better part of junior high?" Would she be so amazed that he could then say "And oh yes, in that other universe, you and I have been married for many years, some of them blissful, the most recent pretty awful, and I take full responsibility, and so hey hey hey whaddya say?"

Vern had lived through it, and it still sounded cracked even to him.

So he arrived early, scored the perfect seat with a view of the water and oncoming sunset, and cranked through Pacificos, trying to take the edge off. But there's a fine line between pleasantly, courageously buzzed and blindingly blotto, so he ordered some oysters, too. Vern, as we know, once had the misfortune of spending some time in California. In California, the oysters don't come with saltines and cocktail sauce. Horseradish sometimes. But mostly a vinegar concoction and no starch. And if you ask for crackers they look at you like you just shit the banquette. But here in Sawnichickee, he could have all the beer-absorbing saltines he wanted. Had the young painter from the garden party been present, he would have been compelled to capture this still-life: sweaty beer bottles standing guard over a pile of plastic wrappers, crumbs scattered across the table.

The beer and the half-shells did their work. Vern relaxed. His story started to make more sense as he ran it on repeat in his mind. Even more affecting than the meal was the humidity. The humidity made everything deliciously languid. Vern languidly relished the languid dusk and the languid sound of languid Gulf waves, the languid gait of the ancient bartender, and the whole languid scene accompanied by a languid duo performing a languid Allman Brothers cover on acoustic guitar and steel drums.

And that's when D'Angelo slid in across the table.

"How do, Vern?"

Vern froze, the proverbial deer in the headlights.

"Working up some liquid courage, I see," D'Angelo said. "I get it. At some point, we men will inevitably have to have an uncomfortable conversation with our significant other. It may be something innocuous like 'if you don't let me put my lips on your toes, I'll have to leave you,' or as countervailing as 'I've been sleeping with your sister for the last fifteen years,' or as well-intentioned as 'you really should try not to talk so much.' Oof. I tried that one once, and let me tell you, it did NOT turn out well. You gonna finish that?"

Vern remained motionless as D'Angelo reached across, plucked the last oyster from the icy plate, and slurped it down raw. No cracker, no sauce, no nothing but briny, chewy goodness.

"So I feel for ya, Vern. Because whatever the circumstances surrounding it, a man in any relationship that lasts beyond three or four hours will, at some point, be obliged to have an awkward conversation. This separates the wheat from the chaff, whatever that means in literal terms, in that anyone who can stare the masculine egoist in the eye and be lied to by him and manipulated by him and cast adrift and forgotten by him and still worship him is obviously the one for whom she is intended. Tammy Wynette illustrated this truism with aplomb."

Vern's brain finally rebooted. He took a shuddering breath as his various internal operating systems chugged back to life. He tensed. Fight or flight, right? D'Angelo chuckled.

"Now now, Vern." He stretched—languidly, of course—and in so doing gave Vern a glimpse of the Ruger LCP concealed in his palm. D'Angelo ended his stretch with the pistol under the table, pointed at Vern's jewels.

"I come bearing glad tidings, Vern, no need to go all rabbit on me. You're headed back!"

Vern blinked.

"That's right. I'm here to take you home. Right now. So, big bonus, that means you don't have to have this doomed chat with your ladyfriend. Trust me, shit with your gal gets a bit more 'you know' when you have to bring in string theories. Moreso when these theories are being laid out by a man, no offense, with only a rudimentary understanding of basic earth science, forget quantum physics. So. Shall we?"

"No."

For the first time ever, Vern had surprised D'Angelo.

"I'm sorry, Vern, did I hear you correctly? Did you just tell me 'no'?"

"Yes."

"Yes?"

"I mean NO. I don't want to go back. I won't. Everyone back there is better off without me."

"That may be true, but that's no reason to stay."

Vern checked his watch. Mia would be arriving any minute. "I have every reason to stay, D'Angelo. Please!"

D'Angelo cocked his head. "I'm sincerely baffled, Bushnell. I thought you'd be happier about this. Thought you might even hug me."

"But I've finally got things put together. I'm moving. Tonight's my last night in the motel. I'm moving into a studio downtown. I'm a rockstar at work."

"A studio? The car wash? Back home you're about to move into the Governor's Mansion in Tallahassee!"

"I don't care! Because here there's Mia! We're in love, D'Angelo. Come on. This is some magical tale. How often? You know?"

Vern couldn't know that D'Angelo did know. D'Angelo knew too well. But D'Angelo had mastered his selfish impulses.

"I've got orders, Vern. You know how this goes. Easy way or hard way, blah blah. But I will say that we should get a move on chop chop, else your wonderful Mia may see you being frog-marched. You want her last memory of you to be pitiful?"

And so it was that Vern's last glimpse of Mia was through the window of D'Angelo's Buick. In her shining face, he saw how she believed the night was going to go. A wonderful date.

A consummation. The beginning of the rest of their lives together.

"Let it go, Bushnell," D'Angelo said, flicking the blinker. "It's truly all for the best."

As the Buick turned the corner, and the tiki bar vanished from view, Vern imagined the next few minutes. Mia's eyes not finding him. Her joy infected by the virus of doubt. The virus multiplying. She sits alone. Drinks alone. Listens to music alone. Tries calling him. No answer; D'Angelo had confiscated his phone and crushed it under heel. Hope holds on: "He's just running late." Fear takes a turn: "Maybe he's in a ditch! Oh god he's in a ditch! Should I call the police?" But ultimately, of course, because the only truly safe place is your tunnel, the virus overruns all. And Mia realizes Vern is just another in her long line of losers. She walks home alone. She cries alone. Falls asleep alone. Wakes to a world that she thinks holds a Vern who has abandoned her, when in fact it's Vernless.

Vern's chest tried to turn inside out. He spluttered.

"Hang tight, Bushnell. Be there soon."

"Can we stop by the motel?"

"What?"

"Just for a minute. One thing I need to do. Please."

"Why? It's a shithole but they do have self-checkout. Just leave the key on the dresser."

"No funny business, D'Angelo. I promise. *Please.*"

D'Angelo sighed. "Oh all right. But only because you shared your oysters."

The Buick detoured. Vern watched out the window, soaking in every last bit of dear, sweet Sawnichickee.

46

CHECKING OUT

Vern felt the cold metal of the Luger pressed against the small of his back. He inserted the key and pushed for the last time into his room at the Spanish Village Motor Lodge. He had already said his goodbyes to the squalid little place, but now that he was being forced to leave instead of choosing to move on up, never had the thin ratty blanket and strangely stained bedside phone and remoteless three-channeled TV appeared so welcoming.

"So why are we here, Bushnell?"

"This is why."

Vern's belongings all fit into one duffel. It sat on the bed. Next to it was the painting, lovingly wrapped in brown paper and twine to keep it safe during the bus ride to his new condo. A ride he now would not be taking.

Vern gestured toward the painting as he scrounged up the paper pad and pen, both imprinted with the Motor Lodge crest.

"Can we please drop this off at Mia's on the way to the wormhole or whatever?"

D'Angelo shook his head. "We're headed the exact other way."

"C'mon, D'Angelo!"

"But hear me out. After I make sure you're safely transferred, I'll make a special delivery myself, alright?"

"Fine. Thank-you."

Vern sat on the bed and scribbled a note. D'Angelo checked his watch.

"You composing a friggin' sonnet? Just say what's on your heart or something."

"What's the rush, D'Angelo? Aren't you and the Project overlords masters of time?"

"Not how it works, Bushnell. You'll find a lot has happened during your absence. But go ahead and get your love note edited all pretty. I'm gonna hit the head. You should, too. Evacuate the bowels. It can get messy transferring otherwise."

D'Angelo saw Vern's radar pinging. Pitiful.

"I thought we'd established a rapport here, Bushnell. Mutual respect. Don't scamper off while I'm taking a dump and make me organize a posse. That's just unseemly."

"I wasn't gonna—"

"You know what, I'll just take this in with me."

D'Angelo hefted the painting and stepped into the bathroom.

"I'll light a match when I'm done."

The bathroom door closed. Vern finished his note. We'll leave it private. No need to pry.

Vern laid back on the bed, idly playing with the pen. He called out.

"Hey D'Angelo?"

"A little busy in here."

"I've been thinking."

"Seriously. Trying to concentrate."

"There's no problem, brotherman. I really don't need to go back."

"OK, so I guess this is how we're doing this. Unbelievable." Vern heard a belt buckle scraping the tile floor as D'Angelo shifted his feet. "It's not your call, Bushnell. Something's gone haywire and they need you back. The reason they didn't just kill you was in case there was a moment like this. So, back you go."

"But I have nothing to offer."

"Be that as it may."

"Not to be morbid—"

"Certainly not."

"—but that whole Queen Palm scene looks a lot like a lost cause. And here? Well, here is a completely different story."

"Lost causes are subjective. Whose cause? Nevermind. I'm not feeling an overwhelming need to discuss your private business. I have my orders, you have yours."

The toilet flushed. The sink ran. D'Angelo emerged holding the painting in one hand and the pistol in the other.

"Your turn. Sorry. No matches."

Vern heaved himself off the bed and went into the bathroom. D'Angelo set down the painting, Zippo'd a cigarette, blew his first drag at the "no smoking" placard on the wall, and called through the closed door.

"Is this all about the peach? The chippy?"

"Her name is Mia."

"Son, I'm sure you've heard about Ulysses and the Sirens. You've gotta get your head on straight. You're going back to wealth and influence. Power up the wazoo. Get yourself a bushel of peaches."

"You don't get it."

D'Angelo snorted. "Oh ho ho. You think you're the first in history who had to hang their happiness out to dry? We all have, son. Yes, even me. I left behind a woman. THE woman."

"Bull."

"All true. I was stationed in France for a spell."

"Army? Air Force?"

"Don't interrupt. This is a good story. I met her in a little village outside Versailles. She made me see the inner layers of transcendence, took away my thirst for fist-fights and rare red meat, made me a better, more evolved person, and put me that much closer to nirvana. But then they moved me to Frankfurt. So off I went. Traded fromage and champagne for schnitzel and beer. I was needed elsewhere. You see? You understand what I'm saying? I was given orders. In this sort of situation, Bushnell, you have to be a goddam man and ditch your bliss and do what you're told."

The toilet flushed. The sink ran. Vern emerged, drying his hands.

"So you see, Bushnell, I've been in your shoes. That pain in your heart will never go away but its profundity will lessen. And by the time you're my age, it will mix and mingle with your sense of impending mortality and guess what? Death will be that much easier to embrace. Now, isn't that comforting? Duty deadens our hearts so we can muster the gumption to get out of bed every morning."

Vern tossed the hand towel back into the bathroom.

"D'Angelo?"

"Yeah?"

"That's horseshit."

"It's wisdom. Gleaned from experience."

"It's just waiting around to die."

"It's self-preservation."

"But preserving yourself for what?"

"The only thing that matters. The end of the foot race. Ready?"

Vern picked up the painting and slid his letter to Mia inside the wrapping.

"D'Angelo?"

"Oh my god, Bushnell, we have to go. When you get back you can join a discussion group."

"How does it feel? The end of the race? Now that you're getting close?"

An ambulance howled in the distance. Vern held D'Angelo's eye.

"If you woke up and found yourself back in bed with that chippy in France—"

"Sophie."

"Sophie. Would you leave it again?"

The ambulance zoomed past outside. The howling siren modulated as it flipped from approaching to retreating.

"Just so you could eventually get around to chain-smoking Dorals, all alone, babysitting people like me, waiting to die?"

The siren faded away. D'Angelo gestured with the gun.

"Let's go. Leave the duffel. Can't take it with you."

47

REALITY IS NOT WHAT IT SEEMS

A voice chirps.

"Sir? Sir are you ok?"

Chirp chirp chirp. It's like he's inside an egg and each chirp pecks. Cracks of light spiderweb the darkness.

"Sir, I'm going to call a medic." Chirp!

Then steps. Expensive wing-tips clipping on tile. Clip clip clip.

"No need to call anyone, he's with me." He knows that voice. Light wriggles in, insistent, and entire pieces of shell fall away.

"Are you sure?" Chirp.

The clips come to a stop, very nearby. "I'm sure, and here's for your trouble."

Large engines rumble by high above.

Vern's eyes open. He sees Cliff Flagler passing some folded cash to the silver-haired chirping volunteer. Hustle and bustle. Garbled PA announcements.

The airport in Queen Palm. It's all the same. It's all different.

He is unborn.

A few minutes later.

"Watch your head there, Vern."

Flagler helped Vern slide into the Escalade. There was another familiar someone already in the back seat beside him, relentlessly thumbing a Blackberry.

"Scott?"

The young aide flinched so hard the Blackberry fell to his lap.

"Hello, Congressman. What a relief we found you."

"Scott Orth, as I live and breath. They let you in on all the secrets, too?"

"They sure did. I've been running interference for you all morning. How was the Appalachian Trail?"

"The... what?"

Flagler lurched into the front seat.

"Your hike, Vern. Your spiritual quest. Scott here knows all about your journey."

The smile on Flagler's face didn't reach his eyes. Vern understood. There were secrets and there were *secrets*. Need to know. Cover story engaged.

Vern turned in his seat toward his jittery, underpaid, put upon aide.

"You're doing a bang-up job, kid. Keep it up. I appreciate you."

Scott's jaw fell into his lap with the Blackberry. Even Flagler blinked.

"And you, Harrison," Vern continued, addressing the driver. "I appreciate you, too."

"The name's Jefferson, Sir." The driver turned in his seat, giving Vern a view of his distinctly non-Harrisonian profile.

"Where's Harrison?" Vern asked.

Flagler answered, "He quit a while back, distraught at your disappearance."

"Distraught, huh?"

"Terribly so."

Scott piped up. "He wanted to join the search party and everything."

"I see."

There was an awkward, silent beat. Jefferson intervened.

"I just want to say, Sir, that I am honored to work for you. I've voted for you every time, and so did all my friends, and we'll vote for you again."

"What for?"

"I'm sorry?"

"What *for*?"

Vern sensed Flagler holding his breath.

"I mean... thank you for your support. I'm lucky to have you on the team."

Flagler exhaled. He tapped the dash.

"Let's go, Jefferson. The Congressman needs to freshen up."

"We'll be at the Ritz in ten."

Jefferson thunked the Escalade into drive and they pulled away from the curb.

"Can we stop at my condo first?" Vern said. "I'd like to see Mia."

Scott squeaked. "Umm, Sir, I thought Mrs. Bushnell was—"

"It's OK, Scott," Flagler interrupted. He locked gazes with Vern. They played tug-o-war.

"Where to?" Jefferson asked.

"The condo is fine," Flagler said. "Seeing home after this long away will do the Congressman some good."

Vern looked out the window. Queen Palm erupted into the sky, alien and familiar.

They arrived at the condo. Flagler rode up with Vern. Scott stayed behind with Jefferson, ignoring his Blackberry's pleas for reprieve.

The elevator dinged. The doors opened directly into that breathtaking view. But the condo was still and stuffy.

"Let me bring you up to speed, buddy," Cliff said.

Vern half-listened as he wandered.

"D'Angelo kept us updated. Things happened here, too. We needed a plausible cover story. Cause and effect."

Vern looked in Mia's closet. Stuff was gone.

"Mia filed for divorce. Florida's a no-fault state. We set her up nicely, don't worry."

Vern looked in his office. It was tidy and fake. A photo-op. He never worked here. He picked up a framed photograph of his mother.

"MaryAnn passed."

This caught Vern's full attention.

"What??"

"It happened quick, buddy. Bryce handled everything. But yeah. It was peaceful."

Vern stumbled to his desk chair, sat, turned away from Flagler, and looked out the window. The teal Gulf waters stretched and yawned. Birds flew by, high above the earth and at Vern's eye level.

"So here's the story, Vern. It's got amazing traction, and if you play your part, you will coast to the nomination. The oil rig explosion, even though you personally had nothing to do with it, caused you great torment, because you care. You're a man of the people. Before you disappeared you even set up a fund for the families of the victims."

"I did, huh?"

"Most assuredly. But the constant, biased, witch-hunt press, plus the grind of the campaign, was too much for Mia. She cut an incredibly sympathetic figure. She didn't blame you at all. She in fact thanked you for your strength and constancy. Want me to replay the press conference?" Flagler reached for the TV hanging on the wall.

"No."

"Suit yourself." Flagler sat on the edge of the desk. "Not two days later, your mother died. Broke my heart, you know how I've loved your family all these years. But the timing, frankly, was inspired. Losing your mom pushed you over the edge. You needed time to reevaluate life, ponder the meaning of public service. So you suspended your campaign and hit the trail."

"I see."

"And now you're back, with a heavy heart and a clear mind and a vision for the future of our great state. Yesterday, when we announced you were returning, donations started pouring in. Our flash polls the last twenty-four hours have been through the roof. And the way you were talking to Scott and Jefferson? Keep up that kindness and empathy thing and we've got this in the bag, buddy."

Vern looked at the Gulf. It was so *big*. The horizon beckoned.

"I'm sure you're still a bit woozy from the whole... transfer-ring whatsit. You've got dinner in a couple of hours with the Sneeds. You want to lie down or...?"

Vern stood.

"Let's go for a drive."

Flagler also stood, suspicious.

"Vern?"

"Humor me, Uncle Cliff. You want me to get my mind right? Let me get my mind right."

"Fine. But don't fuck it up with Scott and Jefferson. Everyone knows just enough to keep this whole thing plausible."

"I got it."

Vern scribbled a list of stops and gave it to Flagler. They rode down. Flagler gave the list to Jefferson.

"No talking," Flagler announced to everyone in the Escalade. "We're giving the Congressman some time to reconnect with his city after his many days away in nature. Scott, feel free to take pics and post to social media. But no talking."

Jefferson drove to the first stop, over the causeway and up the key. Vern got out. Construction equipment and port-a-johns stood guard over the hole where the Azure Tides had once stood. Where, in another universe, it still stood. But here, the hippies hadn't been able to hang on. Wrecking ball beats jukebox every time.

Second stop. Not even a stop. They drove by a strip mall. No New Age-y shop for Sheila to work at. Couple blocks away, no bungalow with blessed access to the Gulf, no firepit, no tool shed splattered with paint. Instead, a white, boxy, gated McMansion strutted in place.

Third stop. His childhood home. No statuary, no life, and a "For Sale" sign in the front yard. He got out, wondered where Bryce was, wondered where his mom was now that she wasn't, wondered how souls worked.

He walked four blocks. The Escalade crept behind him.

The stately, preserved home and carriage house were there. Were the marine biologists inside? And who inhabited the carriage house? Dare he knock? Just for kicks?

No.

Vern stared up at the carriage house door. He wondered if D'Angelo had kept his promise and delivered the painting. If he had, then it would probably be sitting right there on that porch right now—whatever "now" means—waiting for Mia to come home from her shift at the Azure Tides. He stared, trying to see through the layers dividing this universe from that, wondering how many others existed in between those layers, how many Mias were happy, how many were with Verns, how many... how many... how many...

A hand fell on his shoulder.

"Time to go, buddy. Let's go make you Governor."

48

GRASS FED AND DRY AGED

Three perfectly seared and marbled ribeyes appeared on the table. Sandy and Malcolm tucked in. Vern poked at his with a steak knife, trying to muster an appetite.

Sandy's lips glistened. "We are sorry for the inconvenience you endured from our sending you away. We felt it best to keep you out of sight until things settled down. We thought it was the right move at the time."

Vern nodded. "Of course. Enough said."

Malcolm swirled his wine. "Enough said?"

"Yes."

Malcolm made a throaty sound that could have been a "huh" and took a dainty slurp.

"Well, good," Sandy said. "Now, as you surely understand, you are the party's last best hope for this cycle. And everything has, luckily enough, worked out in your favor. From the oil spill to your temporary disappearance, your wife leaving, even your mother—"

"Our condolences," Malcolm said around a mouthful of cow.

"The combination of tragedy and pathos has resulted in the most curious of surges. The primary is foregone. We can start focusing on the general."

Sandy held up his glass. Malcolm wiped his mouth and held up his.

"To you, Vern," Sandy said.

Vern obliged. The three exquisite crystal glasses came together and went *ting*.

The Sneeds re-attacked their meat. Vern contemplated some crusty crumbs on the linen that had made their escape from the breadbasket.

"What would you have done if Lueke hadn't crapped out?" Vern said.

Both brothers froze mid-bite.

"Beg your pardon?" Sandy said.

"If Lueke hadn't died. Would you have just left me there?"

"I don't see how that matters now."

Vern drummed a couple fingers on the table. "Don't suppose it does. It being my moment and all."

"There's my boy. Lueke was merely symbolic. You're our man."

"Always have been," Malcolm grunted. "Always will be."

Vern picked at a piece of fat with his fork. The brothers glanced at each other.

"Now we need you to pull yourself together a little bit," Sandy said. "Eat yourself that steak. Take a rest. Have a shave and a bath. You understand what I'm saying. You have a big ol' day tomorrow. Press conference in the morning—"

"We'll dominate the news all day," Malcolm said.

"—and then a town hall in the evening."

"The incumbent isn't gonna know what hit him."

The Sneeds waited for Vern to respond. Excitement. Gratitude. Something. Anything other than this calm aloofness.

They gave grace for the effects of universe transference, sure, but he wasn't woozy. He was withdrawn. And that was unsettling.

"You hearing us, son?" Sandy said.

Vern shifted in his seat, and for the first time looked the brothers in the eye.

"I was thinking about my old golfing buddy, Dick Swarthmore. You know Dick."

Malcolm couldn't entirely hide the roll of his eyes. "What about him?"

"Remember when he bought that parcel in Nokomis with the animal sanctuary on it? A realtor friend of his had buddied up with the right folks and bought out the landlord and Dick was all set to build a mall or some shit, and he wanted the animals cleared out?"

"I remember," Sandy said. "So?"

"So the sanctuary said that they could not possibly evacuate the premises until they'd found a place for the animals they had on hand. So ol' Dick did what any good businessman would do. He paid to have all the animals transferred to another facility."

The brothers nodded and spoke in tandem. "Of course."

"Except there was no 'other facility,' and here's where it gets weird. Dick had all of those wild animals euthanized and stuffed and he keeps them in his home. His walls and shelves are covered. It's a zombie zoo. He gloats over them like he was the one who bagged them. And I guess he was, essentially."

Time tiptoed past. Malcolm waved off an approaching waiter. Sandy leaned forward and steepled his fingers.

"What's your point, Bushnell?"

"No point, sir," Vern said. He lifted his glass again. "I won't let you down."

49

VERN MAKES HIS PLAY

The remnants of the steaks were cleared. Key lime pie appeared. Vern loved key lime pie. He found that he was suddenly quite ravenous. He reached for his fork, but the noises of unbridled pleasure made by the Sneeds as they took their first bites make his stomach churn. A few seconds later, his pie gone, Malcolm looked up and pointed at Vern's dessert plate.

"You gonna?"

Vern shook his head. Malcolm snatched Vern's pie, inhaled it, and moaned. Vern suppressed a shudder, and left as the brothers interrogated the bill item by item.

"Where to, Sir?" Jefferson asked as Vern got into the Escalade.

"The Ritz."

"Yes, Sir!"

Why not the Ritz? Vern thought to himself. What better place to spend his last night in this universe, and quite possibly in any universe, than in the lap of accustomed luxury? But it wasn't so much the thread count of the sheets or the view of the water. It wasn't the complimentary chocolates or high-end toiletries. It wasn't even the perfection of the Old Fashioneds made by the crinkly-eyed, joke-cracking mixologist at the pool-side restaurant and bar.

It was the courtesy phone in the lobby.

No one had yet entrusted Vern with a new cell phone. He was now a puppet. He could feel all their hands stuffed up inside him. The entire dinner his mind had worked it out. He didn't know about god or God anymore, or even about morality. What did those things mean in the face of so many universes, so many selves? Could randomness exist side by side with mathematical necessity? Infinite monkeys at infinite type-writers till one banged out *Hamlet*... did that mean *Hamlet* was still art? Did that mean Vern had any sort of obligation to himself? To his universe? To the others?

No matter. He couldn't fix other universes. He couldn't even assume they needed "fixing." But what about this one? Could he "fix" it? Or at the very least make amends for what he perceived as wrongs he had committed against it? Or was he just jonesin' for revenge? Ends and means. Outcomes versus intentions. That blistering pavement on the road to hell. Did any of it matter, when the only thing he knew to be true was that when he and Mia kissed, everything made sense? Or more precisely... while with her, it didn't matter that nothing else made sense.

So why not let it rip.

He snuck down to the lobby at 2 am, hoping—praying?—that Gail Hite of ABC-7 slept with her ringer on. Lo and behold, she did.

"Whoever the fuck is calling me at this hour, it better be worth it!"

"I think you'll find it's more than worth it. This is Vern Bushnell."

"Congressman!" Vern heard her scrabbling out of her bed. "To what do I... I mean, what can I do for you?"

"Gail. Listen to me closely. I have to be quick. You'll want to record this."

"OK, OK, OK." A few tense moments as she grabbed her digital voice recorder and got set up. "Congressman, I'm recording. Where were you really these last several weeks?"

"It's funny you should ask, Gail. But here's the deal. Later today at my big morning press conference—"

Gail was breathless. She could tell her life was about to change. "Yes?"

"—I'm going to say some... things."

"Yes??"

"Things that will make a lot of very powerful people very incredibly angry with me."

"YES???"

"They will get so angry, that I will likely disappear again. But this time for good."

"Oh my god."

"And there will be another cover story. I've lost my mind and been committed. I've decided to sail around the world. I've been abducted by aliens. Something so huge and unbelievable that everyone will have no choice but to believe it."

"A Big Lie?"

"The biggest."

"Holy shit."

"But you won't believe it. Because I'm telling you right now what will have actually happened. So that once they announce their cover story, you can release this recording and blow them to smithereens. Maybe win a Pulitzer or three."

Tension. Everything teetered.

Vern thought to himself, *Saying it will make it happen.*

Gail thought to herself, *Don't pussy out on me now, you fucking parasite.*

Vern took a breath and glanced around the lobby. The receptionist was busy. No one else was around.

"After I say these things at the press conference, these angry, powerful people will have me killed."

Gail practically orgasmed.

"You ready for names?"

Gail whimpered.

"I'll take that as a yes. But I have your word you won't release this till after I'm gone?"

Gail recovered from her afterglow just enough to ask, "But what if they don't kill you?"

"Don't sound so disappointed at the idea."

"No no, I just meant—"

"It's OK, Gail. If I somehow survive the day, which is highly unlikely, I'll give you a follow-up exclusive. Deal?"

Gail felt a multiple coming on. She breathed out "Deal!" before once again losing the power of speech for a few seconds.

Vern spilled his guts. Not just names, but dates and events. Account numbers and passwords and dummy corporations. All the skeletons, whether literally buried or metaphorically closeted. He purged. He confessed. He hung up and went to bed and slept the deepest four hours of sleep he'd ever slept.

Gail Hite of ABC-7 made back-ups of the recording. Then she backed up those back-ups while smoking the best four cigarettes she'd ever smoked.

50

THE SPEECH

If you were to hover above Queen Palm on any given morning, say around 9 am, you'd soon learn to recognize how the traffic snarls "in season," as they say, those months from Thanksgiving to Easter when the population triples as snowbirds and tourists flee the cold and snow up north.

And on this particular morning, if you listened very closely, you'd hear a collective, city-wide *gasp* as Congressman Vern Bushnell stepped onto the stage of his old high school auditorium—no hero like a hometown hero—and approached the bouquet of microphones and began to speak. We don't need to transcribe his actual speech. Just imagine Peter Finch at his frothiest mad-as-hell, or Mr. Smith at his hoarsest I-will-not-yield, or, heck, just picture Vern with half his face painted blue and his kilt flapping as he charged pell-mell at the English bastards.

If you continued to hover, you'd be able to pick out Gail Hite of ABC-7 at her desk prepping several dozen emails, each bulging with attached sound files. But Gail is as good as her word. Her draft folder strains, but her trembling fingers do not yet press send.

And over there you'd see some freshly laid tire rubber striping the parking lot. Not five minutes into Vern's speech, Uncle Cliff had raced away to campaign HQ to quell the uprising.

And if you floated down into the wing, just off stage, you could check out Scott Orth, his expression ghastly, his Blackberry miraculously forgotten in his hands even as it buzzed and beeped and chimed. He's young. He'll recover.

And if you lingered in this wing and looked past Scott, you'd see the Brothers Sneed looking decidedly *not* young. They in fact felt like they were aging in fast forward. Never in their wildest dreams had they imagined Vern possessed this sort of spine. His very spinelessness was one of the key reasons they employed and trusted him so. Let's get a bit closer, shall we?

Malcolm leaned into Sandy's ear. The spittle from his lips wetted his brother's lobe.

"NOW can we kill him?"

Sandy couldn't take his eyes off Vern.

"Sandy??"

"Yes. Get Bill Snowden."

Malcolm stepped away and brutalized his phone with a text message. Sandy clucked his tongue and wondered how many heartbeats he had left. More than Vern fucking Bushnell, that was for damn sure.

51

A SURPRISING ACCOMPLICE

Vern wrapped the press conference and strode away from the microphones. Usually when leaving reporters he'd hear "Congressman! Congressman!" launched at his back by multiple voices. But for the first few steps, it was dreadfully, delightfully silent. He had short-circuited the entire press corps. A lawyer for Sneed, Inc., was shoved out into the breach.

"What the Congressman has just said..." The lawyer looked around for guidance. None came. She had a moment to ponder all the life choices that had brought her to this awful moment. And then the dam burst. Questions catapulted. Pandemonium.

Vern kept walking. He patted the crestfallen Scott on the shoulder as he passed. He veered toward the leathery brothers. Sandy Sneed's pythonesque face was unreadable, but Malcolm's was mottled. Malcolm stepped forward, his mouth leering, his lungs forging oxygen into curses. But before the first "fie" or "plague" or "motherfucker" could launch from Malcolm's lips, Vern planted his hand squarely on the old man's sternum and gave a firm push. Malcolm toppled into the refreshment table. Water bottles and muffins and apples scattered. Coffee splattered. In the momentary chaos, Vern bolted.

He skittered down hallways and caromed off walls and why was it that every door he tried to open was somehow locked?? He sprinted past the trophy case, turned a corner, and descended a staircase at a speed that could have been breakneck, except his feet miraculously landed square on each step.

Vern kept running through his high school. His heart hammered against his ribs like an innocent inmate trying to get the jailer's attention. The familiar sharp smell of whatever it was the janitors used to clean the floors each night triggered flashes of memories. Time collapsed. He was young. He was old. He was alive.

He turned another corner and came to an immediate dead stop. Vern had never met Bill Snowden in person. But there was no mistaking the figure casually standing up from his sip at the water fountain. Crisp suit. Polished wingtips. Perfect movie star graying around the temples.

And cold, flinty, infuriatingly amused eyes.

"Come along now, Congressman," the man who could only be Bill Snowden said in a strangely high-pitched voice. "End of the line, I'm afraid."

The self-preservation instinct hardwired into all living creatures propelled Vern backward. He stumbled. He righted himself. He aimed for another door. He heard Bill Snowden's wingtips clip-clopping closer. He slammed into the crash bar. The door opened!

Vern found himself in an alley where an old Buick sat idling.

D'Angelo flicked his cigarette into some trash cans.

"Om Shanti, Bushnell. Best you step aside."

Vern lunged away from both D'Angelo and the door. A few things then happened in rapid succession. First, Vern's feet tangled, so he tumbled face-first to the pavement. This was fortunate because then a couple of slugs passed through the air he had just vacated and impacted the brick wall across the alley. The little puffs of red dust were like tiny celebrations.

Vern looked back, still on the ground, and saw Bill Snowden approaching, clip-clop, suppressed firearm in hand. He closed his eyes. End of the line, indeed.

But then Vern heard D'Angelo say, "Nice suit."

Bill Snowden turned whipcrack fast but not fast enough. D'Angelo cold-cocked the legendary hitman with a trash can lid. Bill Snowden collapsed onto the ground next to Vern.

"Damn," D'Angelo said. "That really is a nice suit." He retrieved the dropped gun, opened the Buick's back door, and offered Vern a hand.

Vern hesitated. D'Angelo sighed.

"Time is racing in unforgiving circles, Bushnell. You getting in or what?"

Vern grabbed D'Angelo's hand. Upsy-daisy.

"Back seat, Bushnell. Head down."

Vern obeyed. He dove into the back, slammed the door, and laid down like a horny teen on prom night.

"Where are we going?" Vern asked.

"That depends. Where do you want to go?"

D'Angelo eased the Buick down the alley, made a few turns, and joined the late morning traffic. Vern shifted. The seatbelt buckle was jabbing his hip.

"Honestly, D'Angelo, I didn't expect to get this far."

"Yeah, Snowden works quick. Lucky for you he also likes to do things himself. Hands dirty kinda guy. Shoulda used the four goons he brought as back-up."

"Four? Wow."

"Don't flatter yourself. Two were trainees."

"Wait. Did you kill them??"

D'Angelo chuckled. "Nah. Gassed 'em all in their Suburban. Their boss might kill 'em for letting you get away, though, once he wakes up. You didn't answer my question. Where do you want to go?"

The buckle kept finding soft spots in Vern's side.

"Can I sit up now?"

"Sure. We're clear. They'll be forming a search party. You have a phone?"

"No."

"Good. Nothing to track. That's why I love this ol' Buick. Built before cars were computerized and infected with GPS."

Vern sat up. Queen Palm meandered by. The sun spit darts of heat at him through gaps between condo towers.

"Why are you helping me? You *are* helping me, right?"

"Don't get squishy, Bushnell. I admire what you did back there. I listened on the radio. Took balls."

"That's it?"

"That's not enough?"

They stopped at a red light. Their eyes met in the rearview mirror. D'Angelo looked away first. He lit a cigarette, cracked his window, and blew some smoke out into the exhausted air.

"What is it G.K. Chesterton said? You can put your head into the heavens but not the heavens into your head? See, I get that. I've jumped between so many universes that now I know more than I should, but less than you'd think. And it's gotten to the point where my brain isn't always sure what it's actually experienced, what's inferred, what's intuited, what's invented."

Vern shook his head. "That is just... far out, man."

D'Angelo smoked and drove. "I think if God is a consciousness capable of perceiving all the universes simultaneously, then said God surely went insane eons ago."

D'Angelo finished his cigarette and flicked the butt out the window. He lit another.

"You do realize I'm still awaiting your choice of destination, Bushnell."

Vern chewed his lip. "You say you know more than you should."

D'Angelo nodded.

"Do you know if Mia will give me another chance?"

"You mean the Mia who tends bar at the Azure Tides back in Sawnichickee?"

Vern nodded.

"The Mia you stood up two days ago?"

"Well you sorta had something to do with that, now didn't you?"

"All I know is that I left your package on her porch. I hung around, cuz I was curious. She got home. She opened it. She looked super angry. Then she read your note. She cried. And she took the painting inside."

Vern squeezed his eyes shut.

"Can you send me back?"

"Will do, buckaroo. No guarantees, but you've got Sheila on your side to help smooth it all over, yeah?"

"Yeah."

"So you've got a puncher's chance."

The Buick made a navigational adjustment. They drove. D'Angelo smoked.

Vern said, "I've only seen one other universe. You've seen how many?"

"A lot. Too many."

"Is it exciting?"

"It's boring as hell."

"No way."

"Look. What I do is basically surveillance. And surveillance is notoriously boring."

"Even across the multiverse?"

"Especially across the multiverse. It's confusing. You forget which damn universe you're in. There are just so *many* of them, which means the differences between them end up being microscopic unless you push out to the extremes. I've seen some messed up shit, Bushnell. But for the most part, surveillance is surveillance. And the power I initially felt from being so in the know? That went away quick. Wandering other universes made me understand just how small each of us truly is. One thing I've realized? The similarities between universes tell far more truth than the differences."

"The similarities, huh?"

"Bet yer ass."

They drove. The sun climbed.

"You know what I can't stop thinking about, D'Angelo?"

"What's that, Bushnell?"

"The Pontus Supreme B-15."

"Why's that?"

"Does it always blow up?"

"Not always. But usually."

D'Angelo glanced in the rearview mirror. Congressman Vern Bushnell was openly weeping.

"How am I supposed to live with that, D'Angelo? All those souls. Burned alive just so a dime-a-dozen politician could have a half-assed spiritual awakening? What kind of fucked up nonsense is that??"

D'Angelo shrugged. "Survivor's guilt. You're not the first. You won't be the last. Humans crave narrative and meaning. I let that shit go a long time ago." He flicked the butt out the window and lit another.

They drove and drove. D'Angelo smoked. Vern cried himself out.

"D'Angelo."

"Now what?"

"What will you do after sending me back?"

"You really care?"

"I really do. I'm at least interested."

"After transferring you back to your Vern-less universe, thus making it Vern-ful, I'm going to smash every record in the lab, knock Emerson and Larchmont's heads together and kick 'em out, douse it all in gasoline, and set it ablaze."

"Holy shit. Really?"

"Yeah. It's time. I'm done."

"What about the Sneeds?"

"They don't exactly accept resignations."

Vern snorted. "Tell me about it."

"But I've got a safety deposit box and go-bags squirreled around. I'll disappear. Not quite the way you will, but still. I've got half a dozen fake names and maybe a dozen good years left. Plenty of cushion. They'll be too busy handling the fallout from Gail Hite's bombshell to worry about finding me, anyway. Smart move calling her, by the way."

"You know about that?"

"Yeah."

"*How?*"

D'Angelo scrunched his brow. "I'm not sure. I just do. I can see it and hear it. Same way I knew to be waiting for you in the alley. Inference. Intuition. Invention."

"You're omniscient."

"Holy shit, I hope not."

They drove. D'Angelo smoked. Vern realized they had exited Queen Palm proper. He looked through the rear window at the receding, sun-blistered skyline. He turned back around and looked out the windshield. Traffic was light. The Buick accelerated.

"I can't wait to see Mia."

D'Angelo grunted.

Vern squirmed. "How much further?"

"Call it eighty, ninety minutes. You want music?"

"No. But hey. After you burn it all down and disappear, where will you go then?"

"I dunno. Somewhere fun where I don't have to watch what anyone else does."

They drove. Time raced in unforgiving circles, around and around.

The past is a present you've already unwrapped.

Vern said, "You should maybe go to France."

D'Angelo smoked. He flicked the butt out the window.

"Maybe I will, Bushnell." He lit another. "Maybe I will."

The Buick purred up the highway, passing undeveloped parcels and skyscraping palm trees. The cigarette butt stayed behind, smoldering on the shoulder. A salty breeze dissipated the meager smoke. That breeze had begun a couple miles west, where the waves caressed the coastline like a finger down a lover's arm. Further out in those teal waters, the mass of black oil floated unaware. Above that oil, huge clouds hung. Beyond those clouds, the sun watched over all.

The earth turned its back. The stars awoke. The Gulf reflected their light.

Infinity glimmered.

52

SHORT STACK

A season or two passed. Maybe a year? Honestly it can be hard to tell in Florida. The leaves don't change colors or need raking. No one has to shovel snow off their front stoop or salt their patch of sidewalk. There's maybe a week or so when the thin-blooded residents dig scarves and lined jackets out of their closets and gleefully go "brrrrr!" as they pass each other on their constitutionals and errands.

This was not that week. But time had definitely passed, the sun hopscotching over our continent's dangling peninsula day by day.

And so it was that morning light dappled by oak leaves and palm fronds eased through the pane glass and across the wall. It groped its gentle way to the edge of a canvas, then playfully walked its fingertips onto the paint, tracing the brushstrokes.

A baby in utero. Eyes open.

The morning light sensed space and leaped from the painting to Mia's face, warming her lashes and tickling her awake. Her lids fluttered open. Her other senses roused. She felt the bed empty beside her, but the pillow wasn't cooled yet.

She smelled brewing chickory. She heard a pan sizzling and an adorably off-key voice softly singing.

I want to put on
my my my my my boogie shoes
Just to boogie with you

She cat-stretched and rolled out of bed, feet into slippers, arms into robe. She scuffled to the kitchen while tying her hair up in a messy knot that she knew would drive the humming man wild. She leaned against the door frame and watched him scoop some batter.

"You're making pancakes."

Vern Bushnell glanced back at Mia. A dollop of batter clung to his chin. She saw him see her messy knot. The look in his eyes made her flush.

"You weren't supposed to wake up yet," Vern said. "I was gonna surprise you in bed."

"I'm surprised."

He went back to scooping. She slid in behind him and kissed the back of his neck.

"But I hate pancakes, Verny-baby."

"I know, but I'm putting crickets in these. You'll love 'em."

"But is that bacon?"

"Yes, dear."

"I hate bacon."

"I know, dear."

"Coffee?"

"Mm-hmm."

"Ick. Blech. Yuck."

"I know, I know."

"And freshly squeezed orange juice? In Florida??"

"I know you hate it."

"*Loathe* it."

"Liar."

"It's just..." Her hands probed his robe. "I'd rather have you for breakfast."

"How much torture can one man take?"

"If I weren't so hungry for cricket pancakes I'd tie you to the rack right now."

"Curse my culinary genius!"

Mia turned with a dramatic huff and flounced away. "Bring it all with you to the lanai, farmboy."

Vern chuckled, readjusted his robe, and flipped a pancake.

Later, syrup-streaked plates and warmer-brimmed mugs completed the pastoral still-life of Vern and Mia simply watching the morning.

Down below, they saw the mailman pull up. He could put the handful of envelopes into the box easy enough from the front seat, but he got out and waved instead.

"Morning, folks!"

"Morning, Lloyd," Mia and Vern replied together.

"Late breakfast?"

Mia grinned. "Late night."

Vern raised his mug. "You know how it goes, Lloyd."

"I surely do, I surely do."

Lloyd opened the mailbox, retrieved the outgoing, slid in the arriving, closed the box, lowered the little red flag.

"There's supposed to be some sort of cold front coming in."

"That right, Lloyd?" Mia said.

"Yep. Could get down into the 70s. Be sure to bundle up!"

They all chuckled.

"Nice looking out, Lloyd," Vern said.

Lloyd looked around and took a deep, healthy breath.

"I tell ya. If this isn't nice, what is?"

They all nodded.

"You folks have a good one, now," Lloyd said as he got back into the mail truck.

"You, too," Mia and Vern replied together.

Later, the plates and mugs dried in the rack by the sink. Another bout of torture had finished with all secrets revealed. Mia was in the shower. Vern descended to get the mail. He waved to the marine biologists as they drove off to work. He flipped through the flyers and envelopes and spied a postcard tucked in. He held it up.

On the front was a photograph of the Eiffel Tower with the words "Wish You Were Here" in red along the bottom. Vern turned it over.

Bonjour, Bushnell.
Take heed. You'll never be free of yourself.
Wherever you go, there you are.
Kind Regards, D'Angelo

Vern smiled. He looked around, Lloyd-like, and took a deep, healthy breath. He listened.

Two chittering squirrels chased each other up a tree.

Butterflies wobbled by, winged giggles.

A distant dog barked. Another distant dog answered.

Bluejays hollered at each other up in the canopy.

Leaves waltzed in the shushing breeze.

And the Gulf waves whispered their timeless secrets.

53

A CHALET OVERLOOKING THE SEINE, RIGHT NOW

So. I actually don't know for certain that Vern is making pancakes for Mia. How could I? I destroyed the jazz lab, remember?

And while that postcard is a nice touch, how could I send it? Neither snow nor rain nor heat nor gloom, sure, and no offense to Lloyd, he seems like a stand-up guy, but how's a courier supposed to swiftly complete their appointed rounds if the sender is in an entirely different universe than the sendee? Interstellar stagecoach?

But hey. It costs us nothing to imagine the possibility. After all, mathematically speaking, with all those Verns and Mias out there, there necessarily must be at least one pair pouring syrup together. Now whether it's "our" Vern or not...

This hurts my brain. It's like my memory is Swiss cheese and someone has filled in the holes with Reddi-Wip. Jam in the nozzle and squirt away.

Here are the only things I know to be true, right now. I'm standing on a balcony in Paris, looking out over this river that has inspired so many Impressionists. I'm wearing a ridiculously luxurious smoking jacket. It cost a bundle but is absolutely worth it. The air is brisk. Behind me, back in the tumble-rumpled California king in the master suite's master bedroom, I can hear Sophie stirring. She's the sexiest damn septunogernian you ever did see. Widowed twice over, luckily for me. And when I walked right up to her in the market yesterday, bold and terrified, her eyes took me back sixty years in a blink. And boy oh boy howdy did she see me, too.

She's calling me back to bed. Y'all've been great. But priorities.

Go get yours.

ACKNOWLEDGMENTS

All gratitude to Sam's brother Mickey, his partner Nicole, and his mom Terry for making this book possible.

Thanks to Josh and Adam.

Thanks to the Rabbit Room, who weekly through lockdown gave Sam mindblown feedback and kept begging for more adventures of Vern and Mia in the multiverse.

Thanks to all the beta readers and volunteer editors (especially Von, Amanda, Denee, and Doug), and to all the folks who voted on the cover.

And thanks to you, Reader, for intertwining your imagination with Sam's. Such acts keep those we love—and have lost—close.

A BRIEF HISTORY OF SAM MOSSLER, IN HIS OWN WORDS

1975. Sam Mossler is born with every intention of leading a pragmatic and moderate life and never referring to himself in the third person.

1979. Sam writes his first masterpiece, *The Eagle and the Ark*, a salty modern retelling of Noah's Ark. Kept under wraps by parents owing to its being politically provocative and generally illegible.

1980. Awarded the role of a lifetime, Peter Rabbit, but complains that the role lacks the complexity and pathos of Mr. McGregor. A character actor is born.

1984. Begins formal theatre training at Florida Studio Theatre. Under the tutelage of Kate Alexander, he learns about emotional accessibility, subtlety, and earnest process. Under the tutelage of Dana Helfrich and Kris McGaha, he learns about pratfalls, double takes, triple takes, spit takes, slow burns, and double-talk.

1989-1993. Attends the Sarasota School of Visual and Performing Arts. Learns a lot. Plays mostly old men and priests.

1993. Enters Florida State University. Things get serious.

1996. Spends a semester in London studying the classics. Begins to dream in iambic pentameter. Gets a gig singing with a Dixieland band.

1997. Graduates from Florida State University with a BFA in Acting and double minors in English and Binge Drinking.

1998. First glorious regional gig. *Death of a Salesman* with Gil Rogers, Jacqueline Brooks, and Apollo Dukakis.

1998-2001. Shakespeare, Chekhov, Brecht, Simon, Barry, etc. in New York, Connecticut, Indiana, Florida, etc. Full immersion in the life of a stage actor. With plenty of bartending in between.

2002. Sam's Chekhovian satire *The Ghost of Firs Nikolaich* is produced in three separate venues in New York City.

2004. Nascent gray hairs and wrinkles begin to emerge. His "type" approaching fruition, he decides to venture through a few smaller markets en route to a huge market, Los Angeles.

2004-2008. Teaches playwriting and acting workshops at public schools across the state of Florida. Unsurprisingly, he learns far more than he imparts.

2008. Arrives in Los Angeles... just in time for the recession.

2009-2014. Nascent gray hairs and wrinkles become less nascent, as does his muse. Completes three screenplays, a stage play, countless shorts, and one or two love letters.

2015. Sam's screenplay *Og's Utopia* gets him an invite (and a Producer's badge!) to the prestigious Austin Film Festival where it soars clear to the semi-finals in the comedy category.

2016. Sam's next screenplay, *Walter Ruddy in Repose or The Green Flash* makes the second round at AFF but ultimately lands with a resounding thud. Positive notes include words like "engaging," "whimsical," and "Wes-Anderson-esque." Negative notes include words like "drooling," "pretentious," and "unsalable."

2017. Sam, like so many Americans, spends the first few months of 2017 in hibernation, not entirely certain that reality as he (or anyone) knew it was as it was. January and February are spent playing Candy Crush. Then Sam writes another screenplay, *The Solfeggio Project* (which became *Queen Palm*). Someone on the Blacklist says it has "en evocative, tremendously smart premise" and is a "formidable, affecting work from a decidedly unique author" and gives it a 7 rating. Then someone else on the Blacklist says "with a rewrite, the script has a lot of potential" and gives it a 6. And yet another Blacklister says "it might be a bit too political for the risk-averse major studios." But the year isn't a total wash. Sam reaches level 338 on Candy Crush and loses thirty pounds.

2018. Having adapted to this proto-dystopia, Sam channels his inner Bourdain and appears as "Chef George" in Will Snyder's *How to Use a Knife*. He also adds another Type-A New Yorker to his resume as "Lawrence Garfinkle" in *Other People's Money*.

2019. Started the year in good company! *The Curious Incident of the Dog in the Night-Time* at Florida Studio Theatre. Fed his soul teaching playwriting and acting to children and adults. Spent a lot of time behind the bar creating craft cocktails and making more Old Fashioneds than anyone should ever have to make.

2020. The year was oozing with profundity. *The Nether* by Jen Haley, who apparently he partied with in L.A. but never spoke to. Then the titular role in Jeffrey Sweet's *Kunstler*. And then the goddam Coronavirus. THIS is why we can't have nice things.

———————

Learn more about Sam Mossler and his legacy at KeepEvolvingPlease.com

Printed in Great Britain
by Amazon

13589200R00155